Praise for *A Mouthful of Air*

"[A] smart, sensitive first novel."
—*ELLE*

"Koppelman nails every detail."
—*The Boston Globe*

"*The Bell Jar* for moms."
—*East Bay Express*

"This is a story so convincing that never again will you pass a new mother on the street without wondering what's behind her mouthful of smiles."
—*The New York Observer*

"[Amy Koppelman] does a tremendous job conveying the point that, although Julie is surrounded with some degree of affluence, none of it can pacify the mental anguish of depression… The mood of the novel is a clear insight into the depth of talent Koppelman possesses as a writer."
—*BookReporter*

"This searing and honest first novel offers both compelling narrative and stunning insight into the crippling grip of depression."
—*BookWomen Magazine*

"Koppelman's prose is as spare and powerful as poetry."
—*St. Petersburg Times*

"Lean, minutely details, and frighteningly convincing."
—*Publishers Weekly*

"Koppelman draws her audience in and never lets loose."
—*ROCKY MOUNTAIN NEWS*

"This new writer should definitely be considered a rising star."
—*BOSTON HERALD*

"*A Mouthful of Air* is powerful, accurate, and insightful."
—*BODY & SOUL MAGAZINE*

"[A] novel that quietly builds suspense to the last page."
—*DALLAS MORNING NEWS*

"Amy Koppelman tells an ultimately harrowing story, but guides it with restraint and honesty, and no small amount of courage."
—*LILITH MAGAZINE*

"Written with a dreamlike intensity... Koppelman is unwaveringly honest and graceful in her storytelling."
—*WILLAMETTE WEEK*

"Anyone who has suffered from depression will recognize the distant, almost ethereal rhythm of Julie's days."
—*KIRKUS REVIEWS*

"So visceral is Koppelman's prose, the reader truly feels the depth of Julie's spirit and the toll of her continual struggle to keep herself afloat."
—*BOOKLIST*

"In this riveting and disturbing novel, Koppelman speaks for women... whose internal battles pass unremarked by society at large."
—*CURLED UP WITH A GOOD BOOK*

"Amy Koppelman offers a message of compassion as well as a scathing indictment of modern American life from a fresh, wholly original angle."
—HOLT UNCENSORED

"A well written, harrowing story (told with glaring honestly)."
—BOOKLOONS

"*A Mouthful of Air* evokes two classics of pre-feminist writing from the last 19th century: *The Yellow Wallpaper* by Charlotte Perkins Gilman and *The Awakening* by Kate Chopin."
—NEW YORK FREE PRESS

"This debut novel is nothing short of astonishing: read it and weep."
—YONA ZELDIS MCDONOUGH, AUTHOR OF *THE FOUR TEMPERAMENTS*

"Eminently worth reading."
—DR. MORTON I. TEICHER, *NATIONAL JEWISH POST & OPINIONS*

"This is a novel to share with a colleague... It is a story that reminds us to care deeply about our patients."
—NANCY GLIMM, C.S.W., *PSYCHIATRIC SERVICES*

"*A Mouthful of Air* is a stunning first novel, which offers no hope to alleviate the pain of despair. The joy is all in Koppelman's gift in telling a true and moving story."
—MAUREEN HOWARD, AUTHOR OF *FACTS OF LIFE* AND *NATURAL HISTORY*

Books by Amy Koppelman

A Mouthful of Air
I Smile Back
Hesitation Wounds

A MOUTHFUL OF AIR

Amy Koppelman

Two Dollar Radio
Books too loud to ignore

Books too loud to Ignore

WHO WE ARE TWO DOLLAR RADIO is a family-run outfit dedicated to reaffirming the cultural and artistic spirit of the publishing industry. We aim to do this by presenting bold works of literary merit, each book, individually and collectively, providing a sonic progression that we believe to be too loud to ignore.

TwoDollarRadio.com

Proudly based in
Columbus
OHIO

@TwoDollarRadio

@TwoDollarRadio

/TwoDollarRadio

Love the
PLANET?
So do we.

Printed on Rolland Enviro.
This paper contains 100% post-consumer fiber, is manufactured using renewable energy - Biogas and processed chlorine free.

Printed in Canada

100%   **PCF**   BIO GAS   PERMANENT

SOME RECOMMENDED LOCATIONS FOR READING *A MOUTHFUL OF AIR*:
Pretty much anywhere because books are portable and the perfect technology!

AUTHOR PHOTO→
Courtesy of the author

COVER PHOTO→ by Becca Tapert
on Unsplash, https://unsplash.com/
photos/4N4WdAJHxcU

First published in by MacAdam/Cage in 2003.

For Brian, Samuel and Anna
and for Diane

"The Girl"

So close to the end of my childbearing life
without children

— if I could remember a day when I was utterly a girl

and not yet a woman —
but I don't think there was a day like that for me.

When I look at the girl I was, dripping in her bathing suit,
or riding her bike, pumping hard down the newly paved street,

she wears a furtive look —
and even if I could go back in time to her as me, the age I am now

she would never come into my arms
without believing that I wanted something.

        —Marie Howe, from *What the Living Do: Poems*

A MOUTHFUL OF AIR

ONE

She is now, to any casual observer, simply another young, tall-ishly attractive girl in a fur-lined leather coat walking across Broadway. A small grocery bag hangs from her left wrist, dark sunglasses and an olive green cap shield her face. Here she goes, pushing her baby's stroller across Broadway, turning left onto Amsterdam.

Julie is alive. Each breath biting at the cold air in front of her this December day is proof. She rests the bag, filled with imported peaches, by the side of the carriage, pulls the wool blanket up past her baby's chin. He is sleeping, his pacifier bobbing up and down in his mouth. Tomorrow is his first birthday, and for breakfast she'll serve him peaches. Puréed peaches. It is 1997, almost the end of 1997, and twenty-five-year-old Julie Davis smiles at each of these thoughts, grateful to be a housewife.

Julie hurries up the hill on Seventy-Seventh Street. Why, she asks herself, do I always forget about this hill? None of the other streets are steep like Seventy-Seventh. She takes a mouthful of air, holds it, releases. This is something she learned at the hospital. If she wants to be a wife to Ethan and a mother to Teddy, she must allow herself to breathe.

"Almost there," she mumbles, the awning of her building finally visible. She is trying to get back before Raymond comes on duty. Most people she is able to face, but Raymond, Raymond is hard.

Julie can picture the plastic oxygen mask pressing against her face, and the awful uncertainty in the elevator man's eyes. After that, she remembers very little about that day other than black.

"Raymond asked how you are again," Ethan told her the night before last while she brushed her teeth for bed. "He wants to know if he can visit you."

"I'm not ready." Julie was surprised by the nasty tone in her voice, "I'm sorry Ethan, I just—" but her husband had already turned his attention back to the television. She looked at herself in the mirror, drawn face, watery eyes. "Damn you." She placed her toothbrush in its holder. How many does Raymond make? Dad, Ethan, Teddy, Raymond, how many lives has she broken?

Forgive. This was another thing they stressed upon at the hospital. If she wants to be okay she must learn to forgive herself. She is thinking about this, her desire to be okay, as the light turns green and she crosses Columbus Avenue. Isabella's patio chairs are gone, boarded for winter. The café's frosted awning a stoic reminder to every roller-blader and coffee drinker on the West Side that spring will come eventually.

Julie sticks out her tongue. She can taste the snow in the air. Its sweetness lingers in her mouth like melted cotton candy. Snow. What does the park look like with snow, she wonders, feeling bad that before all this she never bothered to find out. She stops herself; it is enough already, enough feeling sorry. After all, she is strolling her son down the street. She is, in fact, getting better.

Julie tries to appreciate everything before her: this tree, that passing car, the pretzel guy up ahead on the corner. She has, for whatever reason, been given a second chance. This winter she and Ethan will walk around the reservoir, maybe even go to the skating rink. This winter Teddy will ride high on his father's shoulders, waving his hands, building memories. *Yes*, Julie smiles at the thought of her little family, *there is time again for all of that.*

Still, she isn't blind. She catches peoples' glances, hears their whispering, but that's okay. She'll just keep doing what she's been doing, crack a joke when it gets uncomfortable. "You should see all the consolation cards Ethan got. At least the next time he'll know how many to cater for."

It's hard to believe but people laugh at that. People, Julie has learned, like death in small doses, sputtered between bons mots and bites of capered salmon. Some gesture, a card, a "call me if you need me." But for the most part people don't really want to know the *why* of it. *Why*, after all, has implications.

Even Ethan keeps the wondering to himself. Is it fear? Who knows, maybe it's just his good manners. He was raised in a home where a man and woman, once committed, don't question. Where quarreling, if any, takes place behind closed doors. His mother and father celebrated their latest anniversary on a large cruise ship headed for Alaska. Confetti, an endless supply of crème caramel. It's probably better that he hasn't asked. How's a guy who comes from that, even a guy as smart as Ethan, going to understand why?

Why? Julie knows why. She talked about it earlier in the day with Dr. Edelman and just like her doctor promised, the bottom didn't fall out when she said the words. She said them, cried, wiped her eyes and it was over.

The medicine she's been taking is some kind of miracle. She feels so much sturdier already. Who knows, maybe one day she'll feel strong enough to explain it to Ethan. Why? Because I don't deserve you, don't deserve this kid we have, don't deserve this life you've given me.

She glances at her hands on the stroller. Bumpy pink scars brand her forearms, marking her surrender. She is learning to wear them this way.

With every handshake she reveals that she wanted to die. At least, she thought at the time, at the moment just before she pressed the blade into her skin, at least I will no longer be a liar. And it's true. She isn't just another pretty liar anymore, is she? Is she?

Julie draws back the hood of the carriage. Teddy is so beautiful, so— *A mother's body is no place for a sinner to hide.* She raises her chin toward the sky. Fuck you, she wants to scream but doesn't. Instead she waits a moment; the tears pass. Then she walks, the ten or so remaining steps to her front door.

TWO

The elevator shouldn't take but a minute. Julie passes her hand across the sofa's red velour upholstery. The lobby of her building has a staid elegance to it. She fingers the piping. Celadon, who thinks of that? Celadon and red, just brilliant.

Of course, her mother thought she could do better, Park Avenue, more gilding. But Julie felt comfortable here. Even on the West Side, she explained to her mother, one needs letters of recommendation and tax returns to get accepted into a co-op.

Ethan did most of the talking at their board interview. Julie listened, as transfixed by her husband as the men were: Yes, it was an exciting time for both of them. He had recently been made the youngest partner at his law firm. He specialized in entertainment. No, he didn't know Cruise but Julie taught one of his kids for a few months. Yes, it was a very respected nursery school. They looked in her direction. She nodded.

Did Ethan think Tom Cruise was gay? "Absolutely not. Next question." Travolta? "Don't you want to know if we're planning to renovate?" They laughed.

It was touching to Julie, watching Ethan's repartee with these guys. He had made it. He was no longer another young man to pull for, but everything these men were: bright, successful, a Democrat. He reached for her hand, "And I feel I must tell you because my beautiful wife's not showing yet, but she's pregnant with our first child." Julie nearly died, but oh, how they loved that. Yards of smiles and congratulations.

Julie hears the rumble of the elevator and checks her watch. In a way, by the end of that interview, "Welcome to our building, Mrs. Davis," she too had arrived. She was no longer her father's daughter, but Ethan's wife. The man she married believed, believes still, that faith alone is enough to make anything happen. "This," he's assured her again and again, "is the happily ever after part of your life." Maybe. Julie reaches for the stroller and stands. Maybe it can be.

The elevator doors open. "Let me help you, Mrs." Hector hurries to take the bag of peaches from her hand but stops himself. "That's okay, I got it, Hector." Julie can tell by the shyness of Hector's touch, the creeping stillness of his body reacting to hers, that he is nervous. Imagine, she thinks, pushing her sleeping son into the elevator. I make people nervous.

She's famous now, just like Philip Roth, the writer, who lives on 16. This afternoon she happens to be traveling up with Roth. Roth smiles. She smiles back. Once, ages ago, he offered to give her a car ride downtown, but she was alone then, alone and without baby.

Julie stands straighter, pushing a bit of loose hair behind her right ear. What is she to him? Another Jewish princess riding up a manually run West Side elevator? Another artless girl hiding behind a baby carriage?

She can feel his troubled eyes on her body. Does he know what she did to herself? Julie glances at him but he doesn't give back. Anyway, she thinks, he's too tall, isn't he, too tall to love?

Yet she wants to. If he could see beyond what she appears to be, if he gave her the chance, she'd know how to love him. His large nose, glasses, leathery skin. They could help each other. She could hold him against her chest, rub her fingers through his thinning hair. Yes, at this moment Julie is sure that if Philip Roth gave her the chance, she'd know how to love him.

But he won't find me attractive, not now, not as a mother. Julie feels herself begin to sweat and loosens her scarf. This scrap of herself so vain and ugly is what wraps itself around her shoulders at night. Here it is again, waving a finger. Its foreboding voice warns: *You are going to fail, you can't help but fail.*

Julie is aging. The girls in the magazines and the football players at the Super Bowl are younger than she is now. So she worries, despite the love of a husband, despite a baby who beams at the sight of her, what will happen when her beauty is gone?

Ethan assures her again and again that he won't leave. He does it all the time. Little mentions of it here and there. He points at old couples shuffling down the sidewalk, carries on about driving cross country in a Winnebago one day, tells her she's pretty, even prettier than the day he married her. Maybe he won't leave.

But her father left. All those years later, all those promises whispered among the three of them, and still he left. Fine, maybe Julie has a chance. Maybe if she works real hard at it she will be able to forget him, or at least be able to rid herself of his constant presence. But what prospect is there for her mother, forty-eight years old, two grown children, a grandmother?

It's not like Julie can pass her mother's number to Phillip Roth. The guy would take Mia Farrow because she is, after all, Mia Farrow. But other than her and maybe a select handful of additional women, he'd insist on someone younger. Youth assures unadulterated love, or if not unadulterated exactly, certainly something easier on the eyes.

So here is Julie. Smack in the middle of her own drama. Punching through life with diaper cream in hand. She is as ready to live, to believe, to purée peaches, as anyone on the verge of ·happiness. But what if none of it, the therapy, the Zoloft, the understanding of her past, will stop her from ending up alone?

Look at Roth. The guy's fairly neat, his tweed coat fitted, a folded newspaper under his arm. But in the end aren't all men the same? So what if he's a writer? His face, her father's.

He talked softly as the back of his hand passed over her cheek. She held her cone up, looking for approval and he nodded. It's Kohr's Custard, Haagen Dazs, Carvel. It's all that ice cream. He licked his thumb, his breath stale from whatever it was he ate the night before. He wiped the extra vanilla away, keeping her mouth clean. He smiled at her, supporting her decision to continue. She bit into the cone and when it dripped, when she lost control, he was there, with another napkin, with his moistened thumb. They continued this way. Year after year, cone after cone, until she became fat.

Men, Julie is certain, have countless chances. A man is never too old to make a baby. For a man it's never too late to find a new little girl to love. Hector opens the elevator doors at five. Julie looks one last time at Roth, bows her head, then backs herself and her sleeping child out of the elevator and into the hall.

THREE

Georgie greets her with a sigh, a genuine sigh of relief. "Where were you?" Teddy's nanny asks.

"At the fruit stand on Broadway." The fruit stand sounds good to Julie's ear. Strolling your kid over to a fruit stand, buying a couple peaches, can't lock you up for that.

The two women stand on either side of the door, a sleeping baby between them. This, as nice a moment as any for Julie to say something. But how, how does one go about thanking someone for saving their life? *It's a good thing you came to work early that day, or, Geez, Georgie, I would have bled to death if it weren't for you?* And then what, follow that up with a hug?

"The man have nice fruits at that stand."

"Yeah, he had really nice peaches today." Julie holds out her bag of peaches. *See, I really did go to the fruit stand.* Sure, she brought it on herself, *what do you expect when you slit your wrists?* But she'll figure it out, figure out how to mend things with Georgie. What's that saying? Keep your friends close, your enemies closer.

"Can I come in?"

"Oh, sorry, Mrs."

Georgie steps back, allows Julie to push the stroller into her foyer. What she'll do is, she'll buy her a gift. It's perfect, Julie will meet her mom at Bloomingdale's. Her mom will know what to choose, a new winter coat, a sweater with a bird theme, a pretty filigree cross. Yes, she'll buy Georgie a gift, wrap it real fancy. Hallmark doesn't make a postsuicide thank you note, but there'll be something close.

In fact, she'll follow up the shopping with lunch. Her and her mother back at their favorite diner, an egg-white omelet, a Diet Coke. Eventually, if she works hard enough, this whole little episode will sink into memory. Yes, there will always be the scars on her wrists but with time they'll fade. Julie will be another person who made a mistake but she'll be alive. Not much different from most people really.

Teddy makes a noise. What does the little guy want? Both women reach for him. The boy looks to his mother and then to Georgie. Georgie turns to Julie and smiles. Under a different set of circumstances it would be a look-how-cute-he-is smile. But today's smile isn't saying that. Julie rests her arms on the side of the carriage and waits for Georgie to scoop up her son and carry him away. *How*, she wonders, as she watches them turn the corner, *how did I lose my little boy to a stranger?*

Julie looks around her apartment. Barbie dolls, jelly glasses, snowglobes. Undoubtedly, other people collect this shit; Julie's not the sole member of the Lunchbox Association of America. Still, in order to get better she must accept that these various collections aren't decorating choices alone. She's not some ten-year-old with a dollhouse.

She's an adult. She should be collecting china or candlesticks. Something with purpose. There's no way Georgie would waste her hardearned money on stuff as frivolous as this.

Salvation. One thing's for sure, if there's such a thing as salvation it's certainly not at the bottom of a Snoopy thermos.

"Depression has many faces," is a big one at the hospital. Yep, Julie thinks to herself as she runs into the kitchen to answer the phone. This time it came into her kitchen wearing a farm theme, kittens and cows on hand-painted tiles, a black-and-white checkerboard floor, strawberry paper. Who knows what it will be the next time. With so many different motifs to choose from, the possibilities are endless.

Julie is not sure if this is funny or sad but it's the truth so she tries, at least, to understand it. And what she's slowly beginning to acknowledge is that her depression, God does she hate that word, her sadness, her melancholy, this wish of hers, to shut her eyes in the hope of everything fading to black, is not something that's ever going to go away. There will be times that it will subside, a happy Sunday, a few happy Sundays. But be assured, it will come at her again.

The hope is that with hard work and a bit of luck she'll be ready. After all, she's got the shrink, the meds, fucking live in help.

Julie lifts the receiver off the hook, "Hello?"

"Hey, Tiny." Her husband's voice is soft, easy.

"Hi," she says, cradling the phone against her ear.

"How 'bout a game?"

"A game?"

"I'm not pressuring you or anything. If you can't do it, you can't do it. But Ira asked if we could join him and Robin at the Knicks game tonight, and I thought, why not try it."

It takes her a minute. She looks at the strawberries; a happy person doesn't paper their entire kitchen in bright red strawberries. "Tine?" A smaller strawberry print covers the ceiling.

"Tine, all I need is a yes or no."

She remembers the last time, all those people in one sealed space. "I'm sorry, Ethan. I want to go. Didn't I say that? I want to go to the game."

"That's great. And don't worry, if it's too much we'll leave early."

Julie knows that Ethan's lying. There's no way he's going to get up and leave, not the kind of fan he is. Nevertheless, the enthusiasm in his voice makes her feel good. Julie wants to be able to do this, give her husband a night at the ballgame.

"Where should we meet?"

"Meet me inside the Thirty-Fourth Street entrance. At the escalator. I'll be waiting for you."

"Wait. What time?"

He laughs, "Seven-thirty."

"I'll meet you there." Julie is excited.

"Where?"

"Come on, Eth. I might be a little depressed but I'm not an idiot."

"You're right. I'm the idiot. The idiot with a big smile on his face."

Julie hangs up the phone. For a moment she can't seem to locate her hands. They feel as if they are hanging off her arms, fatty, numb appendages without bones. She shakes them out and grabs a cigarette from the cookie jar on the counter. That last game was well over a year ago. Maybe tonight won't be as bad.

"I'm running downstairs to get the mail," she shouts to Georgie. Since the "accident," Ethan insists on calling it an accident, Georgie has been living with them in the small room off the kitchen. Julie doesn't like it but it shouldn't surprise her. What was Ethan going to do, quit his job and stay home with Teddy while she figured out how to get a grip?

And Georgie is trustworthy, she'd been cleaning their apartment since they moved in so it makes sense. There's more than enough room for her. In fact, the real-estate agent referred to the room Georgie's living in as a "maid's room" when she showed them the place.

At the time, Julie was taken aback by the term "maid." She couldn't believe people still used that word. No, she insisted, if they bought the apartment that extra room would be an office for Ethan, or a nursery for their second baby. She wasn't the kind of person who had live-in servants. She laughs to herself. She's certainly that kind of person now.

Georgie's only here until you get better. Maybe Ethan's being sincere when he says this. Maybe he believes that she will get better. But what does that even mean? Will better be when she can give her son a bath without fearing she'll drown him? Sure, that will be better, but better enough? She'll still have to feed him without him choking to death, change his diaper without causing a urinary infection.

Fuck it. There's nothing she can do other than what she's doing. Yesterday the dry-cleaner, today the fruit stand, tonight the Knicks game. Still, it doesn't seem fair, like she should have to worry about thanking Georgie. Julie pushes open the door to the back stairwell and kneels between the two large garbage pails. She lights her cigarette, takes an empty Coke can out of the recycling bin and tips her ashes into it. Why is she hiding out here when through that door is her son, her home, her strawberry wallpaper?

Before Julie got pregnant with Teddy she would look out her window and see these young mothers pushing their Perego strollers down the street. They always seemed to be giggling as they passed. Julie couldn't wait for Teddy to be born. She did everything she was supposed to: stopped smoking, took her vitamins, ate properly. Finally, there she was, another mother walking down the street with the same Perego stroller.

"Somehow," she told Dr. Edelman, "I got the stroller, but not the giggle."

Julie hears footsteps above her head. Someone is coming down the stairs. She takes a long drag before dropping what's left

15

of her cigarette into the Coke can. The last thing she needs is for the Super to find her here, report back to Raymond how it's true, how he saw it with his very own eyes, that crazy Mrs. Davis, perched like a bird on the stairwell, sneaking a smoke.

But it shouldn't be this way. Cigarettes shouldn't be something Julie should have to sneak at her age. *For Christ's sake, millions of people smoke.* Julie laughs, to picture them, Raymond and Hector, Owen the Super, to picture them congregating around the boiler, eating their bologna sandwiches, gossiping. *Why she not happy, the girl in 5B?*

I have become a fool. Julie washes her hands in the kitchen sink. She towels them dry, lifts her fingertips to her nose to make sure they smell clean. *I have become a* Cosmo *article.*

Julie looks through her kitchen window. In the apartment directly across the courtyard a simple chandelier glows above a small dining table upon which a single plate, a single glass, a single teacup is set. Ivory curtains, pinned back on either side of the window, rest at the edges of a lime green linoleum countertop. *Sad,* Julie thinks, *that little old lady all alone.*

She checks the time on the microwave. She really should start getting ready, but the peaches. She opens the paper bag. There they are, still round and fuzzy, not a single bruise.

Away, she envisioned coming home and puréeing each of Teddy's meals, baking him cookies in crisp star shapes, scrambling him eggs. Julie wants Teddy to grow strong, to be a fine young man. A young man whose boxers stick out of his chinos as he walks easily, tall and thin in a faded T-shirt.

Julie still remembers the good little things her father did: how he sliced her bagel evenly, right through the center, tied her shoes in double knots, made her laugh, loved her. "Sometimes," Julie whispers into the air, "sometimes you make me feel like I'm in mourning."

Julie leaves the bag of peaches on the kitchen counter and walks down the hall. She will be able to do lots of nice things for Teddy. For now, though, she must shower and dress and meet her husband. Later, she tells herself, later she'll boil the peaches.

FOUR

Your tits. Your tits sag. Sometimes darkness gives that voice too much space. Julie opens her eyes, hoping that the light of the bathroom will make it go away. *Your tits sag like a monkey's nip.* Julie steadies herself, lets the water drain down on her.

Georgie will only let the shower run for so long before knocking on the bathroom door with one of her, "You okay, Mrs.?" So she doesn't have much time; Julie needs to condition her hair, shave under her arms. She leans against the rose-colored tiles and slowly eases herself down to the floor. "Your tits sag, Harriet." She hears her father saying the same words to her mother, "Your tits sag like a monkey's nipple."

Julie focuses on the tepid water puddling between her legs. Her mother never seemed to pay him much attention when he said these kinds of things. She simply carried on with whatever she was doing at the time. Julie pictures her mother setting her hair in large plastic curlers, a silk robe, a slight sloping of her breasts. Her father passes by them, tight white underwear, long muscular legs, a knowing little laugh and then, "Your tits—"

Julie pushes at the glass. The cool air from the bathroom makes her feel better. She pulls herself up and out of the shower, wraps her body in a towel, diverts her eyes from the tub as she has trained herself to do, and walks into the bedroom.

"What did Daddy mean?" Her mother continued to roll even sections of her hair into the large plastic curlers, "Ma?" But it was only after each and every strand of hair was bound tight to her head that Harriet responded. "I guess," she said, biting her lower lip, "I guess it means that he doesn't love us anymore."

Julie sits on the edge of her mattress, head bent, hair draping over her face. That wasn't true. The din and heat of the blow dryer comfort her. Memory, she reminds herself, isn't a trick. Her father still loved her then, still shaved her legs, brushed her hair, painted her toenails. She must stop feeling guilty. It isn't her fault that he didn't love her mother anymore, is it? No, she's been through this a million times; of course it isn't her fault.

More importantly, Ethan likes her tits. In fact, the night before the "accident," one tit in his mouth, the other cupped in his hand, there he was with, "My God, I love your tits." Yes, she reminds herself. Her husband's voice, not her father's is what she must listen to.

She turns off the blower and flips back her hair. Who should I be tonight? She walks over to her vanity and rests her hand on a pale blue glitter shadow. Glitter? No, she sorts through her colors, stopping at a compact of brown tones. Tonight she'll return to the Garden as the young mother. She will paint her lips a nice rosy bee-stung color, maybe a gloss.

Julie removes the makeup from the drawer and places it on her vanity. A light blush might be nice or a little rouge. She glances quickly at herself; she looks clean and scrubbed, younger than she remembers. "Okay," she says out loud, "you can do this."

Julie has finished getting ready. She is wearing a loose black shirt, jeans, boots. Everything is covered, her ass, her wrists. She even has a few minutes left to play with Teddy. She walks into the living room. Where are they? She's about to panic but then she hears noise coming from the kitchen.

There's her boy, kicking his legs in his highchair.

"You look nice, Mrs."

"Thanks, Georgie." Julie brushes the back of her hand across her son's forehead. How great is this: her boy mushing peas back and forth in his mouth, gumming his food like an old man, "So we should be back around—"

"I know, Mrs., I spoke to Mr. Ethan."

"Oh." Julie feels like a child. Did he clear the game with Georgie when she was out getting the peaches or did he wait until she was in the shower? *How's my adorable boy? Still adorable. And my crazy wife?* Julie stops herself. Time, things will get back to normal, she just has to give it time. After all, it's only been a couple of weeks.

"You like to feed him?" Georgie asks, gesturing the spoon in Julie's direction. Still, the nanny's capable hands taunt her. "No thanks." Julie waits for Teddy to swallow and then kisses the top of his head. "We have to get you a haircut, my love." He looks to her, his eyes wanting. "Don't worry, I'll be home soon."

Julie walks into the foyer and takes her coat out of the closet. Who's she kidding, I'll be home soon. Teddy's not worried about her coming home. He wants his food, his bottle, a nice warm bath. It's really too dark for sunglasses, but there they are on the console. Julie grabs them. Wearing sunglasses at night will make her look like an asshole but she doesn't care. It certainly won't be the first time.

"See you later." She closes the apartment door behind her and presses for the elevator. These are the moments that seem ridiculously hopeless to Julie. "A spoon," she will tell Dr. Edelman tomorrow, "of all the things in the world to fear, I fear a spoon." Julie hears the rumbling of the elevator coming to get her and remembers Raymond. *No, not tonight.*

Back in the stairwell Julie listens. The elevator doors open, then close. Everything around her is gray: the floors, the walls, the railing. Next to the garbage pail is the Coke can she used earlier. She lifts it off the floor and tosses it back into the trash. She looks at her kitchen door and then presses her ear to it. She wants to hear Teddy laugh, happy little boy.

"Hey, Julie."

Julie jumps. William, the teenager who lives in the apartment above them, is walking toward her, his arm hanging over a girl's shoulder. They are making their way down the stairs, William in his Yankee cap, the girl in flared jeans, platform boots.

"Spying on the baby-sitter?" His smile is warm, almost merciful.

"You caught me." Julie tries to relax her voice, to sound peppy, as if it's par for the course that she should be alone in the stairwell with her ear pressed against the door. She looks in the girl's direction.

"This is my girlfriend, Charlotte."

Julie pushes her sunglasses up over her eyes. "Nice to meet you, Charlotte."

The girl grins, proud she is of her guy, of the way he wrestles, of their prom in the spring. William takes a joint out of his pocket.

"My mother used to do that," he says as he lights it, "used to spy on me all the time." He takes a drag without coughing and shares it with his girlfriend, who takes a drag and hands it back.

"We're going to see Phish over at the Beacon." He waves the joint in Julie's direction, "You want?"

"No thanks, but I'll walk with you down the stairs."

"Great."

She trails behind them, all geared up for William to stop, to turn around and ask her what happened. His mother, nice woman, baked her a pie, must have said something to him. Perhaps he was late that day and saw the ambulance on his way to school. Who knows what he knows. The point is Julie's ready. If he mentions it, asks her what happened, well, she'll just be cool about the whole thing. "I pulled a Cobain," she'll answer him, "Cobain in Rome."

The three of them make their way down the stairs, William and Charlotte casually passing the joint back and forth. Near the bottom, William snuffs out the flame with his thumb and forefinger. "Nice night," Charlotte says as they walk outside. William squeezes his arm around her waist. "Yeah, babe."

At that moment it all seems so clear to Julie, how it happens that one becomes what she herself became. She waves her arm in the air for a taxi. Look at Charlotte, another girl in the midst of her beginning, outfitted with shiny hair, a handsome boy, and her fair share of a tightly rolled joint. Another girl ill-prepared for her future?

What the fuck do I know, Julie thinks as the taxi pulls to the curb. Maybe Charlotte's as self-assured as she looks. "Have a great time, guys." They wave.

Julie opens the taxi door, slides into the backseat, "Thirty-Third and Seventh, please." She turns around; through the rear window she sees them slowly making their way down the street together. She wishes she could thank them, thank William for not fearing her; thank both of them for believing in a night at the Beacon.

FIVE

Julie sits in the back of the taxi, counting pizza parlors. Forty-five, she guesses, forty-five pizza parlors to the corner of Thirty-Third and Seventh. No, forty-nine, forty-nine pizza parlors. This is another hospital thing. Not counting pizza parlors exactly but the idea that if Julie finds herself in a situation that frightens her she should try to transfer the fixation, reassign her fear. So forty-nine it is, forty-nine or so pizza parlors to the corner of Thirty-Third and Seventh.

"Tell me when you see a doughnut place, lady." Julie checks the guy's license: Sal Adrianni 12B05. "Don't mean to scare you there, hon. Just see you back there looking out the window and it's my night to bring refreshments." He points to his list of AA steps on the dash. "Yep," he continues as they stop for the red, "seven days."

Sixth Avenue will break at Fortieth and then it's no more than five minutes to the Garden. Julie rolls down her window. This guy's not going to hurt her, just wants to talk. "Congratulations," she says as politely and with as much volume as she can muster. The light turns green. The city air, as refreshing as it is dirty, presses against her cheeks. *I'm okay*, she reminds herself, *everything is okay.*

Julie travels downtown, fighting to assemble the memories that swirl around her head. She and her brother are quietly eating eggs. Their father is reading the paper in his pajama bottoms. Their mother is upstairs, sedated with Valium. Eight pizza parlors, zero doughnut stores.

Julie travels downtown, clutching a glittered heart doily she's just made in school. Her mother is out of bed today; she's driving Julie and her brother to Dairy Queen. There's Mom, her long hair escaping through the car's open window. "I've got clouds in my coffee, clouds in my coffee and," Julie hears her mom singing. "You're so vain. You probably think this song is about you. You're so vain…" How she wanted to be like her mother then. Twelve pizza parlors, still no doughnuts.

Julie travels downtown, unleashing time. All those lonely nights waiting on the stairs for her father to come home only to leave him for Ethan. She was the one who left first, wasn't she? Ten more steps: she's scared she might trip. Seven more steps: she starts to cry. Five more steps: she begins to believe in safety. Two more steps: she sees Ethan reach out his hand. One more step and they stop. Her father lifts her veil. His kiss warm and wet with loss.

Daddy, she hears herself saying as a young girl, *promise me you'll be the one to carry me over the threshold?*

Julie shakes the memory off, presses her body into the backseat. She looks at the guy's list of AA steps. Her brother should go to rehab or AA, get a good look at what twenty years of hard living does to you. Julie's tried. She used to say to him, "David," there he was with that big red bong, eight in the morning, eleven at night, "David, you need to get some help."

But what leverage did she have? He didn't give a shit about serving doughnuts. He'd smile, say something like, "You're sweet, Jule." Sometimes though, especially after a little go-round with coke he'd get nasty, "Easy for you to say. All you had to do was get married."

Julie never takes any of it personally. David grew up wanting to be a rock star, he's in a band, plays a mean guitar, maybe it will happen for him. Still, Julie thinks, even if he's able to triumph, land the cover of *Rolling Stone*, headline Wembley. Even with a hundred thousand kids cheering his name, he'll never feel loved.

Look at her. Isn't she nearly everything she had hoped to be? A girl with just enough taupe shadow on her eyes, a hundred-dollar bill in her pocket, a husband, a son. *Big fucking deal.*

Why? Why can't she keep this bitterness, is it bitterness, out of her head? She married Ethan for his decency, had Teddy thinking love could be pure. It's not. Twenty-eight pizza parlors. Eight Ray's, one Ray Bari, one Sbarro. Still no doughnuts. *It's just not.*

Finally she sees one. "Stop, okay?" Her speaking voice is pleasant.

"What, miss?"

"Pull over." In fact, Julie likes this voice, all sing-songy and confident.

Mr. Sal Adrianni pulls over. "I'll be right back." Julie jumps out of the cab, leaving the door open behind her. Sal puts his car into park and watches her hurry into the doughnut store. Inside he sees her talking to the young guy behind the counter. He can't hear her but she asks, "Can I have two dozen?"

The guy behind the counter has a cross hanging from his neck, "Two dozen, what?"

"Two dozen of those." Julie points to the doughnuts with pink frosting and colored sprinkles.

"The iced jellies?"

"Yeah," Julie takes a second, compares the ones she's chosen to the simple glazed doughnuts above them, "the iced jellies."

The guy begins filling one box and then a second. The store's fluorescent lights are bright. Julie rubs her hand into her cheek, worried that the base she chose to wear will look caked under the even brighter lights at the Garden.

"You're all set," the guy says. He wipes his hand across his forehead, erasing little pearls of sweat. She takes the money from her pocket and passes it to him. "A hundred's all you got?"

"Sorry." She's a little embarrassed.

"Why buy doughnuts?" he grumbles to the cash register.

Julie doesn't let the guy bother her, though. It doesn't matter what he thinks. She heads back to her taxi with the two boxes of doughnuts pressed against her chest. In victory, she takes her time.

"Here," she offers, tapping the boxes against the passenger window. Sal leans over and lowers the window for her. Up front there are rosary beads, a cinnamon-scented air freshener and a Mets sticker. Julie passes him the boxes. Look at his face, his warm brown eyes, his smile. She's made him happy, hasn't she?

Julie notices a picture pasted on the lower part of Sal's dash. "That your daughter?"

"Sure is."

Close up like this, Julie can see that Sal's lips are chapped, that he has a substantial scar above his left eye, that he hasn't shaved for at least two days. How did he do it, she wonders? Did he rage or was he quiet, did he give her a kiss or not even bother with a good-bye?

You make them, these little girls that you dress up, a white Peter Pan collar folded over a red cable-knit sweater. Two barrettes in her hair, her face cupped between her hands, a black background. There she is smiling for you, the photographer's flash branding first grade. Most of first grade you were gone but now look at you, what a good father you are, driving around with your little girl's picture on your dash, seven days, a couple boxes of doughnuts. Here you are, another lousy Mets fan in recovery.

"She's beautiful. Six?"

"No, seven. Seven years old."

"Yeah," Julie says, remembering herself at seven. She climbs back in and they continue. "Seven's a nice age."

"Daddy," she asked as he picked her up off the top stair and carried her into bed. "Tomorrow can we get the pumpkins?"

"Sure, honey," he answered, his tie undone, his chest hair warm, thick and dark, perfumed. Even his smell she remembers, the lingering scent of his safety. He left her there, in bed, more or less just another girl watching the door slowly creak closed behind him.

He is Superman, King Kong. He is the magician at Becky Macintosh's birthday party. He is Ronald McDonald. He is Daffy Dan. He is, still, her everything.

"We're here," Sal says, gliding over to the curb in front of the Garden's VIP awning. "Not a chance." He clears the meter. Julie puts her money back into her pocket, slow to move. "Make sure you don't forget to give your daughter one." She points to the doughnuts.

For Julie, hope lies somewhere in the center of one of those doughnuts. But for the life of her she can't imagine the enormous leap of faith it would take to bite into one, swallow it, keep it down.

"Of course not. I'll bring her one tomorrow." The guy says this with such utter sincerity that Julie is smiling as she steps out of his car. For some reason it doesn't seem to matter much to her anymore if he's lying.

SIX

The air outside the Garden tonight smells of roasted chestnuts and Christmas time. Julie hears the sound of a horn, a saxophone? She looks but can't find where the notes are coming from. She pulls her sunglasses down over her eyes. It's cold, she thinks, clasping the collar of her jacket, moving forward.

Through the revolving door, she sees her husband leaning against the wall. Ethan smiles when he sees her. He wants it to be this simple, a wife meeting her husband at a sporting event, the difference between winning and losing points on a scoreboard.

"Hey, Jule," he says as he takes her by the hand and leads her toward the escalator. She did this with her father, clasped his hand and followed. Julie remembers the largeness of her father's hands, the steadiness of his palms, the warmth. Her husband's hands are small by comparison, fragile.

"You okay?" he asks as they step off the escalator. Ethan is like this, cautious, kind. They watched a prize fight on their first date, the Super Bowl on their second. Ethan thought he married a girl who was a sports fan. *Well,* Julie grips her husband's hand, *he thought he married a lot of things.*

Together they pass a ladies' room, a hot-dog stand, a bank of phones and a sweepstakes entry booth. There are legs and more legs, sneakers, red crocodile boots, faces. Finally, they reach the gate. From up here the Garden is nothing more than a blur of laughter and denim. Julie takes a deep breath, all those steps. She looks toward Ethan. He is tall, she thinks as they descend, not like Philip Roth in the elevator, but tall.

"Hey, man." Ethan stops and introduces Julie to some old fraternity pal. Stops again to congratulate some other guy he knows on a start-up something or other. While he's doing this Julie breathes and takes inventory. She is at the Garden with her husband. They are making their way down to the firm's seats. They will watch the game, chat at halftime, watch the rest of the game and go home.

She reminds herself that she has done this before; gone with Ethan to see the Knicks play in the Garden, sat courtside, kept her eye on the ball, her arm hanging over Ethan's shoulder, a smile on her face. It's never easy, but she'll do it, chat with Robin, shake hands with whomever at the half. She can be as professional as the ballplayers, as professional as any other wife.

Just then two girls with terrific midriffs pass by. The one sporting a belly ring gives Julie the once-over. The other, in her skintight Lakers tank, looks at Ethan. Julie pulls her glasses back over her eyes. It doesn't matter if they think he could have done better, if they think she's thick in the middle, even fat. Julie sifts her fingers through her hair. Makebelieve, she reminds herself, is easy.

"You're here!" Robin jumps out of her seat when she sees them, "I was starting to get worried." Are they late?

"Who cares what time it is." Ira gives Julie a kiss before she has a chance to check the clock. "The important thing is that you made it."

Julie can just picture it. The two of them meeting up at the corner, preparing themselves. Ira saying something to Robin like, "Don't worry, honey, I'll step in if it gets awkward." Julie shouldn't be so cynical or so narcissistic, for that matter. Maybe it means nothing to them, so she tried to kill herself, so what?

Ira's a founding partner, Robin a trustee at Dalton. They have bigger things to worry about: their penthouse in Carnegie Hill, their place in the Hamptons. And Julie knows better, knows better than to think it's all perfect for them. Everyone has their problems, maybe one of their kids is fucked up, maybe the roof on their building has a leak. Still, it's different. People find a way to cope. Sure, it's never easy, but for most people it's a different kind of hard. Strength of will, Julie thinks to herself, is it strength of will that makes it all work for some people, strength of will that gets you the courtside seats?

Julie looks around. Cross-court she sees Woody Allen in a red sweater, Soon-Yi next to him in a Burberry overcoat. Donald Trump's brother and his socialite wife are sitting to the right, just under the basket. A few seats over Matt Dillon has his arm around Cameron Diaz. Next to them Maury Povich and Connie Chung.

"You want anything?" And there's Spike Lee talking to some gorgeous woman holding Prince's hand, "Honey?"

Julie focuses. A waiter is standing in front of Ethan, taking their order, "I'm okay."

"You sure?"

She looks at her husband. "A Diet Coke."

"Easy." Ethan passes the waiter a ten from his billfold.

Everyone in the place stands. At center court, a Black girl in a red velvet dress with white cuffs begins singing the national anthem. She's twelve, thirteen years old. Her legs are a little short for her torso and she's a bit chubby but the girl sings as if unaffected by any of this. Loud, fearless, her voice bellows with freedom. Imagine, Julie thinks to herself. Imagine being able to do that.

Still, can anyone sustain this level of self-belief? Julie looks at the girl, sure she's young now, and when you're young like that you have faith in tomorrow, faith that your legs will grow, your voice will broaden in range. When you're young like that you are happy with complimentary seats, it isn't a once-in-a-lifetime, isn't charity.

When you're young like that, you believe. Believe that there will be countless chances to stand in the spotlight and shine. The girl finishes, bows, walks off the court. It doesn't seem fair that the girl's moment should be over already.

They sit back down, Ethan passes Julie her Diet Coke and begins eating his fries. He's become heavier since she's been sick. "I love you," he says, taking her hand again. But his "I love you" feels staged. He hasn't told her he's loved her since the hospital. So why now?

She realizes, just then, that none of this is about her. Tonight isn't her return to the Garden; it's Ethan's. *Look at me. I'm with my pretty wife. I'm a well-fed man at courtside.* Julie's stomach cramps. Does he consider himself a failure? She looks at Ira and Robin, do they?

Julie never meant to shame Ethan. How can she explain this: that he's a good husband, a good father? That he never neglected her. That there were no signs, at least no signs he could recognize. Julie thinks of Teddy, of his birthday tomorrow, of his fat little hands. A year ago Ethan held their son as the doctor took him from her. She remembers the look of awe in her husband's eyes. "Is that his head?" he asked the doctor. "Julie, I can see his head."

I guess, Julie reminds herself as she looks at the muscled bodies of the ballplayers in front of her, there are instances of beauty, real beauty. Soon the lights will dim, the players' names will be announced. Soon Julie will have the chance she is waiting for, to bend her head over, wipe her eyes. "Here are your New York Knicks!" The crowd cheers. One by one they enter, big men with fire in their legs.

The buzzer starts the game. Forty-eight minutes on the clock, two and a half hours of actual time. Julie's stomach cramps again. She should have prepared. She should have eaten something at home. There are no safe foods for her here. No hard candy, no dry toast. But look at Blaine Trump, sitting up all straight in her pinstriped suit, legs crossed, alligator shoes. Look at her, married to the wrong brother and still able to eat popcorn.

"All right!" Ethan shouts. He jumps to his feet, fist in the air. "Did you see that?"

"Of course." Julie answers as convincingly as she can, rising in support.

"Really? Even with those sunglasses?" His voice is playful.

"Yes, even with these glasses." She lifts them up over her eyes, smiles, works harder.

"You look beautiful," he says, mistaking her smile for happiness. "I knew you'd have fun."

This, Julie knows, is the answer, is in fact the only answer. She'll just have to keep at it: going to games, socializing at halftime, drinks after the game, whatever it is. But to succeed she must stop resenting what he asks of her. It's a basketball game, it's a beer, it's a little fake laugh here and there. It's not like Ethan's asking her to go work at the checkout line at Waldbaum's. At this point, he doesn't even expect her to cook.

If she can hang on, play the part for long enough, she can right the situation. Julie absolutely has the power, the strength of will, to put everything back together. And she'll do it, just watch, she'll make them a happy little family again. It's easy. She'll go back to the basics. Remember the names of the other wives, their children's birthdays. Send the appropriate gifts; Ethan's mother likes orchids, his sister French hydrangeas.

She must manage the apartment properly. Make sure Ethan's closet is well organized: his shirts neatly arranged, ironed underwear, socks without holes. The refrigerator should have 2% milk and Tropicana Original without the pulp. The freezer, Breyers vanilla bean.

Oh, and his medicine cabinet needs two of everything, two nose sprays, two dandruff shampoos. She'll make sure a box of Kleenex with aloe is beside his bed, that rubber soles are put on all his shoes. The list goes on and on. But that's all it is. It's only a list.

Julie scans the crowd again. There are so many girls, twenty-ish like her, begging for a chance at a successful young guy like Ethan. All these single girls, growing older, losing distance every year. Julie spots one bantering cross-court, flipping her hair off to the side, pretending to be looking for her seat. Is her life better? Is that what Julie would want? If she had a chance to do it all over, would she want to go back there? Go back to being a single girl, digging around the Garden, hoping for a glimpse of Jerry Seinfeld?

If Julie had a daughter she'd drag her to Rome before letting her marry, to Rome and then to Paris if need be. She'd push her to have sex with all different types of men. Maybe if Julie had done that, known her body more. Maybe if her mother had encouraged lovers, a minor-league pitcher, a furniture maker, an artist in the East Village. Maybe that would have made her more secure, more able to handle this life she's gotten herself into.

Julie watches Ethan open the foil of his burger. He looks at her, offering, "You sure you don't want anything, honey?"

How to answer that?

He leans his head out the window, tosses you his keys. Four flights of stairs you must climb to get to him. Four flights that seem like nothing.

You sweat, perspire, in bed, all day, over, beneath, on top of his tangled sheets. You tickle his ear with your tongue, lick off the wax, then bite. You let him bleed, consume his blood, fill yourself.

You watch *Oprah* or an A&E Biography. Share a piece of toast and a cold glass of cheap wine. You're not an alcoholic. You're just hot without air-conditioning. The wine cools you, makes you sleepy.

You wake up startled and want to cry when you realize he's gone. But you don't worry. He returns all wet from the rain, with his dog and two hot knishes. He unwraps one for you, releasing its steam before lifting it to your mouth. You eat your whole knish while his long rounded fingers work the remote, flipping through basic cable. Back and forth and back and forth the same few channels until he finally decides on Arnold Diaz and the Six O'Clock News.

You lay beside him, window open, listening to the rain. You with some dog and your artist boyfriend with the big nose. Funny how you love that nose. How you love to touch it, hold onto it in your sleep, how you'll use it to anchor your dreams. It's all you remember of him twenty years later, as you lie in bed with your husband whose nose is a stranger.

"John-John's over there."

"Honey," Ethan says, interrupting Julie's daydreaming, "Ira is talking to you."

"Oh." Julie turns her attention toward them. "Sorry I didn't realize."

"I was saying," Ira continues, "John-John is right over there?" He points in the direction of Woody Allen's seats.

"Honey," Robin interrupts her husband, "How does Carolyn look?"

"Terrible."

"Really? I can't believe you can see that far," Robin rolls her eyes at Julie. "Amazing, I'm blind as a bat." Julie watches in disbelief as Robin proceeds to take a small pair of binoculars out of her bag. She holds them just above her nose. "This is exciting. If they're out together in public then maybe the rumors that they're breaking up aren't true."

For a second there's no talking. Then, "You're absolutely right, Ira. Carolyn's a mess. Her eyebrows are too thin and her hair is too bleached. She looks like the life's been drained out of her."

Ira nods his head. "Wave, honey," Robin instructs him. "I'm sure if you wave he'll wave back."

"You want to take a look?" Robin asks, offering the binoculars.

"No thanks," Julie answers, trying her best not to sound offended.

Robin moves closer to Julie. "I don't know if Ethan's told you that Ira's become quite close with the family over the past year or two. I could just kick him at times. Just the other night I answered the phone and it was Joe. Joe Kennedy on our phone, calling personally to confirm the date of the brunch we're throwing for him at '21.' You'll be there, won't you, honey?"

Julie nods.

"Anyway, I put the Congressman on hold, walked into the den to get Ira and sat on the sofa, listening to them carry on. Well, when Ira finally hung up, I said, 'Damn you, Ira. If only you'd been able to establish this kind of rapport sooner, we could have been at the wedding.'"

Julie smiles. It's funny really, funny the different things people want. The minutes pass slowly. My God, Julie thinks, looking up at the retired jerseys hanging from the stadium's rafters, there are people that would die for these seats.

"You know," Robin says, placing her hand on Julie's knee, "you know, the big thing now, even more than John-John and Carolyn, is Mother Teresa. Everyone keeps talking and talking about Mother Teresa and her godliness, but I say, 'Would you want to be Mother Teresa if you had to look like her?'"

Julie waits for the play to be completed. "Fly," the guy eating the hot dog right behind them shouts. "Take the ball and fly."

"I guess not," Julie answers.

"That's what I think. That's a big price to pay, even to become a saint."

Julie knows that this inane comment is Robin's attempt to make her feel at ease.

"So," Robin continues. Up close her breath seems warm and slightly sour to Julie. Her lip liner too dark. But these are the only imperfections Julie can find in her. "Are you feeling better, honey?"

Julie looks cross-court at Cameron Diaz, with her long legs and expansive smile. "Yes—" Robin sent Teddy a cashmere baby blanket when he was born, magazines to the hospital. "Yes," Julie repeats, forcing herself to confront the woman's eyes, "I'm feeling much much better."

Robin squeezes Julie's knee and turns her attention back to the game, "Glad to hear it."

"You sure you're feeling better?" Ethan asked that morning. Julie remembers holding Teddy in her arms while Ethan bent over to pick up the paper. "Maybe you should go see a doctor."

"Don't worry. I'm fine. I just get nervous when we leave Teddy." Julie pressed the elevator button for him. The night before they had gone to a cocktail party at the Pierre. Julie had them quit early, but it's not like she didn't make it up to him. They came home, had sex, watched TV.

"It's more than nerves. At the party you said you thought you were going to faint. Why not try a doctor?" Ethan said this matter-of-factly as he scanned the headlines.

"You know my stomach gets funny when I'm nervous, Eth. It's nothing." Julie kissed his cheek. He glanced up from the paper, at her, at Teddy, "I just don't think these, I don't know, anxiety attacks you keep getting are normal and—"

The arrival of the elevator interrupted him. "Good morning, Mr. Ethan," Raymond said as he held the gate of the elevator open. "Good morning, Mrs."

"Hi, Raymond." Julie began waving Teddy's arm up and down. "Say hi to Raymond, Teddy. Hi, Raymond."

"Promise you'll call the doctor," Ethan said, stepping in. "I'm no expert but I'm sure there's something you can take for those."

"Okay," Julie answered her husband as the elevator doors closed. It was eight-thirty in the morning, and the cleaning lady, which is what Georgie was at the time, wasn't scheduled to arrive for another hour. So there was time, not too much time, but time enough for her and her boy to be together alone.

Julie carried Teddy through the apartment and into her bedroom. Sure, Ethan was right. There were things she could've taken, she could have gone on an antidepressant, or popped an anti-anxiety pill every now and then. But it's not like she was some crazy person or something. She got a little nervous when she left Teddy with a sitter, a little tired in the afternoon. What new mother isn't a little nervous and a little tired?

Julie set Teddy down in the middle of their mattress. He could sit up by himself, how damn cute he was, the proud little Weeble. Julie ran around to the other side of the bed, pulled down her sweats and hopped in right beside him. She handed her son his Pooh bear, booped his nose, then slid his feet toward her until both heads shared one pillow.

She remembers gazing at him, this miracle of a thing: his large protective hands. "As long as we're together everything's fine, right, baby?" She tickled her fingers back and forth across his belly. He kicked his legs, opened his mouth.

"Milky?" Julie raised her shirt, eased Teddy's head toward her breast. She waited for his lips to cup themselves around her hardened nipple, but Teddy unlatched himself and looked at her.

Julie's forefinger traced the lines of his lips. He was so beautiful, her boy. She moved her finger into his mouth. He bit down, his gums hard, how they ached for teeth. "What do you want, little guy?"

The boy reached for his mother's face and she responded, curling toward him, pressing her lips against his. They were so soft, so minute, so easy to swallow. She slid her tongue into his milky-tasting mouth. Just for a second or two, just long enough to know that she liked it. She couldn't deny it. She was in love with her own son. She was a pervert.

SEVEN

"I'll be right back, Eth."

"Where you going?"

"I want to get something for Teddy."

"Okay," Ethan hands her his wallet and turns back to the game.

Julie climbs the stairs. It's not as if she's lying. She's going to get Teddy a jersey, she's just taking a little detour first. A cigarette will ease her cramps. If she's lucky she'll be able to find one quickly.

She stops at the landing, checks to make sure her ticket is in her pocket. Maybe the restaurant on the lower mezzanine, they have a bar. Julie scans the crowd. There's Ethan, she smiles. There's her husband, talking easily to his friends, comfortable in his world.

Julie draws her glasses back over her eyes. She wishes she didn't feel this way, didn't feel like the outsider here. But she does, she feels lost. There is, no matter what Ethan says, *his* world. And then there is her own.

In Julie's world, Teddy would be a Nets fan. He'd be forced to root for the underdog. Season after season Julie lay in her father's arms, the television loud, the sherbet cold. "If you can't be loyal to your team, who can you be loyal to?" *What a joke.*

Thankfully, Teddy's growing up in Ethan's world. There he can root for any team he wants to root for, even a winning franchise like the Knicks. It's going to be different for him, lucky little guy'll have Patrick Ewing to bring him home.

Julie checks the scoreboard; tonight should be an easy victory. She looks through the crowd one last time for her husband. There he is, much too far ahead for her to ever catch up.

The child's jersey hanging in the window of the souvenir shop is too big, but maybe there are smaller ones inside. Julie decides she'll do this first and then bum a cigarette. She walks inside the store and is directed to a rack by the window. "So cute," she says, holding the smallest #33 in her hand. She takes out Ethan's credit card and pays.

Back on the mezzanine she heads left for the escalator. She hasn't been gone very long, there's still time to have a smoke. In fact, maybe she'll just tell Ethan the truth, tell him that she needed a little nicotine to calm her nerves.

"Flower."

Don't, she brushes the sound of him off her shoulder. Not tonight, tonight she's going to ignore the echo of his voice. "Julie?" He walks toward her, passes through her. She knows this for certain. How she loved him.

"Daddy," she says almost inaudibly.

Ron is not actually moving. He is standing by the phone booth, knee bent, one foot against the wall, the other firmly planted on the floor. In real life Julie's father is simply another fifty-year-old man dressed in black: black boots, black jeans, black hair again.

She could, she knows, walk away from him. It wouldn't be wrong if she decided to do that. Or she could stroll over and slap him, for leaving her mother, for leaving her and her brother, for not even having the courtesy to say a proper good-bye. It wouldn't be wrong if she decided to do that either.

But what Julie wants to do is walk over to him with her head held high. She wants to tell him that she's happily married, that she loves Ethan, that she's survived. She wants him, her father, to lift her into his arms, to hold her as he had when she was a little girl. She wants him to tell her that it's okay: okay for her to be happily married, to love her husband, to live a life separate from him. And then possibly, if there's time, they can even talk a bit about Teddy.

"Hey, flower," he says, planting a kiss on her left cheek. *Did he just kiss me?* She looks down at the floor, steals a breath. *He can't hurt me*, she tells herself before looking at him. His eyes, she notices, aren't nearly as blue as she remembers.

"How you doing?"

How's she doing? "I'm okay, Dad."

He shuffles his feet from side to side, "You sure looked bad when I saw you in the hospital. You remember me coming, right?"

Julie is determined not to let him make her cry. "Thanks."

"Yeah," Ron looks at the door to the ladies' room, then back to his daughter. "How's Mom?"

"Mom's okay."

"And your brother?"

"He's—"

"There you are, Ron." Julie is startled by the interruption. Is this his girlfriend?

"Just waiting here like a good boy," he says, pecking whoever she is on the lips.

"We really should go back to our seats."

Julie can't believe the size of her. She must have five inches on him. Is she beautiful or just tall? Is she even thirty?

"Sure, honey," Ron says, taking the soaring girl's hand. He looks at Julie, "Take care of yourself," and then he walks away.

"If I'd had you for a mother, my entire life would be different." How bloated and silly Julie felt on the couch in front of him. What was it, a year? Must be a year, little over a year and a half ago that he came over to visit.

"Yep," he said, pacing around the living room of her apartment, dark suit, blue shirt, ever-present yellow tie, "I never really had a mother."

"Why don't you sit down, Dad?"

"No thanks," he said, stopping at an old silver frame. In it, Julie sits on his lap, wearing her best party dress, white patent leather shoes. She is showing off the heart-shaped locket he has just given her, polished and filled with an uncomplicated love. She is five years old.

Julie remembers wanting to lift herself up off the couch. Just like tonight, part of her wanted to run to him, to climb onto his lap, to be that little girl again. But then there was the picture to the left. She's older and he's got his arm around her waist.

"So, Dad," Julie continued, "what do you think we should name him?"

"Him?"

She remembers her father turning toward her, unsure. His eyes tired, glazed. She saw that he couldn't place her, couldn't account for all the time that had passed, couldn't process who she was. Another man's wife. Another man's possession.

"I was hoping it would be a girl."

A quiet passed between them that day. A lengthy, exhausted quiet, his unspoken way of saying good-bye.

He lifted his coat up off the sofa.

"Can I use your phone?"

"Sure." She turned to face the window. She thought he wanted this for her, wanted her to grow up, to get married. She didn't show him the tears in her eyes that day either.

Julie follows her father, watches his head blend with the crowd only to disappear. Again he is one of thousands and again she is alone.

Julie's breath is short. She tries to hold it. Here it is, happening again. She leans against the same wall her dad had been leaning against when he called her name. There is nowhere for her to go. No smoke. No escape. This is all her own fault, her fault for leaving Ethan.

"Honey," a nurse in the hospital told her, "there are only two alternatives. To live or to die."

"I know," Julie said, knowing that it wasn't true. Knowing that she had spent most of her life stuck someplace in between.

He is only a memory.

Julie feels for the ticket in her pocket. There's nothing to do but walk back to her seat. One foot in front of the other. It's as simple and difficult as that.

"Long line?" Ethan asks as Julie sits.

"Yeah, really long. Did I miss anything?"

"Just the dancer and the contest guy. Missed by three feet."

She decides not to tell him she saw her father. Why ruin Ethan's night too? Her husband smiles at her. His two front teeth are white, but they're capped. Sometimes for no reason at all she hates him.

Second half, two quarters. An hour and it will be over. Robin passes Julie a box of Cracker Jacks and watches. Will Julie eat one? Is she better? Julie reaches into the box, picks off a peanut and pops the Cracker Jack into her mouth. "Why do you like the Knicks so much?" she asks Ethan.

"I don't know. I liked them since I was a boy." Julie puts another Cracker Jack into her mouth. Its sweetness whets her appetite. Her belly growls for more but these two bites are enough. She can't do more. More, she'll lose control.

Julie leans in closer. She's happy that Ethan's put his arm around her. How much simpler life would be if her mother was right, "If you look happy and pretty then you are happy and pretty."

Ethan proposed to Julie at his old apartment on Eleventh Street. Van Morrison, dim lights, the whole thing of it all. He knelt before her, his shoulders broad, chest hair dark. There he was, on one knee, the velvet box open, the diamond ring. His considerate eyes pleaded with her to believe that he was different; that he was a man without wants.

Yet it turned out that he did *need* more than to dance with her in a long ivory gown. He *asked* her to love him as he loved her.

The Knicks City Dancers walk out, still smiling even in the face of defeat. So much for the frontrunner, no timeouts left, down by three.

And yes, Ethan still loves her as promised, but today's love is rationalized, an emotion that swells from some misguided sense of duty. If only he'd take her face in his hands and squeeze it, have the courage to shout at her, shake her, make her cry. If he could be honest with her, then it wouldn't seem as ruined. But now he's too scared. He'll never come clean; stubborn man, never admit he bet wrong.

Look at Ethan, his shoulders pressed forward, as if he himself were in pursuit of the ball. Look at him, just thirty, little bits of dandruff on his sweater. Ethan has such a tiny nose. Teddy has the same nose, Julie thinks. The same nose, maybe the same eyelashes. The chin. Maybe even the same chin. Her husband turns his body to the right and smiles at her as the ball whizzes by them.

For the most part what he's lost will go unmentioned. This much she is certain of. His displeasure with her will remain unsaid. But part of it, part of this unsaid, of this hole in their relationship is his responsibility too.

Fine, if he doesn't want to talk about what happened they won't talk about it, that's his prerogative. But it'd be nice if he put an end to his *everything's-going-to-be-okay* bullshit. How's everything going to be okay, it's not like she has some boo-boo you put a Band-Aid on.

She is sure if Ethan met her now he wouldn't marry her. Yes, Julie is convinced that his marrying her was a mistake. One of those romantic gestures people make in their youth. No different than holding a boom box up to a girl's window in the pouring rain. An innocent, Ethan was then. He bought his tuxedo for their wedding at Zellers and paid with cash.

Maybe tonight, when they go home, she'll get him to talk to her. Georgie will be sleeping, Teddy. Maybe she'll even be able to get him to touch her, put his hand on the nape of her neck, drag his fingers down around her breasts, press his lips into the cavity of her chest. If he just gave her the chance to atone, she'd feel that much better.

She wonders, though, if Ethan will ever feel safe enough to really love her again. She knows he will continue, come home from work by nine, eat dinner, watch the late news. They will talk about the son they share, his day at school, his friends. But will there ever be more than that? Will they laugh?

"Tine, you look at all those girls and think you're fat, right?" Ethan points at the Knicks City Dancers. "Well, you are thinner than all of them. I just wish you knew that."

Julie looks at him. Poor guy's trying so hard. Somehow she must find a way to show him how hard she's trying. Tomorrow is their son's first birthday. She must swallow a bite, just a single bite of Teddy's cake.

Surviving the attempt has given Julie a break. But sooner or later people's curiosity will get the better of their fear. People—just like Ira and Robin had—will start calling for plans or Ethan will have a client in from out of town and want her to join them for dinner.

Once Teddy starts school there will be no end to the demands. Julie will have to shake a tambourine, drink coffee with the other mothers, join the nursery school's raffle committee. During this intermission from the various duties of her life, Julie must sort things out, figure out who she is and what she wants. Dr. Edelman asks her this all the time. "What do you want, Julie?" Still, she doesn't know.

But Julie knows what Ethan wants. Ethan wants the girl she was before her attempt, the girl she pretended to be. He wants the life he thought he was saying good-bye to that morning, his delicate wife, their baby boy in her arms.

Julie glances at the clock. There is too much time left on the scoreboard. She slips her thumb under the edge of her shirt and touches one of her scars.

You look at yourself in the mirror. There you are one man's daughter, another man's wife. You fix your bare feet on the cold tile floor and dare yourself to look again. You are also a mother. A mother waiting for her morning bath to set, nipples dripping, sour mouth.

Look at you, liar. You're the one who says you love your husband when maybe it's only a desire to love him, to be loved, to be normal, safe. You're the one who just tongued your son and liked it. You're the one who everyone thinks is so fucking perfect, so fucking sweet, so fucking good.

Fine. Ethan wants the wife and the son. That's fine. He wants to be the handsome man in the Mandarin collar. Sure, she'll try to give him that again. But this time she's not going to fake it.

Julie checks the score. The problem is she doesn't give a shit that the Knicks are trailing by three. This is Ethan's team, Ethan's memories. These aren't the colors she anticipated, not the cheer she hoped for. Even Ethan's clothes don't have the scent of detergent she's accustomed to.

"Isn't he old already, Patrick Ewing?" Julie asks Ethan.

"An old warrior."

A little girl in pigtails sits. Knees curled into her chest, cheering. She looks up at the sky, then at the basket. She marvels at the smoothness of his follow-through. The little girl in pigtails continues watching. She cheers each time he gets it in and even when he just hits the rim. She sits, knees still curled into her chest, admiring his foul shot. Eventually, he becomes bored and drops the ball. "Game over," he says and walks away.

"All right!" Ethan jumps to his feet again. "I told you he'd do it."

The place is going wild. Julie turns around and looks up. Somewhere out there her father's clapping. He certainly has no shame about it, prancing around the Garden like he owns the place.

She left him first. She orchestrated her escape. She chose the date, the time, the music. But none of that, she has to accept, none of that makes her a traitor.

"Let's go home." Ethan grabs Julie's hand. They kiss Ira and Robin good-bye. Lots of *take cares* and *let's get together soons*.

"Go New York, Go New York, Go!"

On the way out of the Garden, Julie and Ethan pass the same two girls from earlier. "Go New York, Go New York, Go!" They are waving their arms in the air. Julie looks at the one wearing the tight jeans and Lakers tank. This is the point, isn't it? Anyone can be a Knicks fan.

EIGHT

The lamp in the living room is on, waiting to greet them. The toys that were scattered about before Julie left are now put away. The chenille throw lies folded on the corner of the couch. The pillows puffed.

Smiles sparkle beneath tidy glass frames. There she is, a bride. There she is again, a mother. Julie walks down the hall. The door to her son's room is ajar, the night-light plugged in, the monitor green. Julie can't help but notice how immaculate it all is. This is what her home is like without her. In Georgie's household everything is in place, orderly and motionless.

Julie watches her son. He is sleeping alone in his crib, combed hair, socks on his feet. He is long and narrow like Ethan. He is his father's son. Julie sits in the rocking chair beside him. Teddy's even breathing soothes her. This is something she knows she wants. It's not too much to ask for, is it? He breathes. She breathes.

Julie looks at Teddy's bookshelf, at his well-organized changing table. She created this nursery, hunting through paint samples until she found just the right pale blue. She chose natural wicker for this rocker, a cherry finish for his crib.

She stands, walks over to Teddy's window, and raises the blind. The Museum of Natural History is right across the street, Central Park on the corner. She'll teach Teddy how to ride a bike on this street. She'll wrap the pedals with paper so his feet can reach more easily; push him into the park like the other mothers. Julie hears the water running for Ethan's bath. She touches the rim of Teddy's crib before leaving the room. *I only missed a month*, she reminds herself.

Julie sits at the edge of her and Ethan's bed. She can't help but laugh. For their bedroom she chose wallpaper with a peonies motif. Bright bunches of pink peonies all over the walls and ceiling, a pink-and-white plaid carpet. *How awful*, Julie thinks as she unlaces her boots.

But it isn't in poor taste. There's kitsch, that's for sure but there's nothing tacky about her home. It's lovely, in fact, light pine floors, country English furniture, carved armoires, needlepoint carpets. What feels awful to Julie isn't the wallpaper as much as who she was when she chose it. *If you look happy, then you are happy.*

Julie stands, takes a step, and knocks on the bathroom door. They've only been living in this apartment for a couple of years but it seems like a long time ago; a long, long time ago since she was able to believe in the color pink.

When Ethan doesn't answer, she eases the door open. Their small bathroom is cloudy with steam and memory. Ethan soaks in the tub, a book between his hands. Julie squeezes a bit of toothpaste onto her toothbrush. It saves him, she thinks as she brushes her teeth. His ability to concentrate, to cancel out the whole world and escape is what saves him. But, Julie wonders, looking at his reflection, she continues brushing, is it possible to compartmentalize pain and still care?

"Hey," he says, putting his book down. Julie rinses her mouth and turns. "Thanks for coming tonight."

"I was happy to." Julie shuts the lid of the toilet seat and sits. She watches Ethan rub a bar of soap over his arms. Oatmeal in his bath, dry skin, he is shy somehow. He splashes water on his shoulders, massages his fingers through his hair. As Julie watches him do these things she is certain that she loves him, that none of what she did to herself in that tub happened because she didn't love him.

Julie holds open a towel as he eases himself up. He steps out of the water, his thighs wide, his dick formidable. He dries himself, then powders himself, then stops to clip a toenail. He brushes his teeth, combs his hair, puts on deodorant. Throughout each task he glances at her with quiet interest.

If Julie had the guts she'd drag him out of the bathroom and throw him down on the bed. She'd tickle him like she used to back in his apartment on Eleventh Street. She'd tickle him until he nearly choked with laughter.

"What's going on?" he'd ask after he caught his breath. She'd be sitting on top of him, her legs straddled over his chest. "I'm better," she'd answer him. But before he could do anything sweet, give her a hug, a kiss, suck her tit; before he could do anything for her she'd already be down on him, her mouth wrapped around his hardness, pulling. If Julie had the guts she swears she'd make him a happy man in that way too. If she had the guts.

Instead Julie decides to walk into the kitchen. She opens the window above the sink. She isn't going to sneak around anymore. This is her house and if Georgie is bothered by cigarette smoke then she can leave. And Ethan? Ethan will just have to understand.

Julie turns the flame higher on the gas stove and lights her cigarette. She first saw this Garland stove in an ad. There it was in the pages of *House & Garden*. Look at those happy children waiting for their pancakes. A five-grand investment in a griddle for Sunday-morning pancakes seemed cheap to her. Five grand to have that kind of happiness. Well, Julie thinks as she reaches for a pot, cooking is the least of it.

Julie holds the burning cigarette between her lips and begins filling the pot with water. She looks around her kitchen and spots the utensil she needs. She shuts off the faucet and places the pot on the back burner. She takes a drag, pulling the smoke in deep. Cigarettes always make her feel better. She releases her breath and watches as the smoke escapes through the window. Across the courtyard the old lady's living room light is still on, the same expectant plate.

"I thought you quit." Ethan surprises her.

"I did," she says, turning from the window to face him. Why does every little act need to be analyzed, every bit of smoke measured? She decides she'll try to charm her husband into releasing her. After all, it's only a cigarette. "Just one to calm down," she says in a light tone of voice, "from the game, the crowd. It got me a little shaky, that's all, honey."

But it doesn't work. Julie can see it in his eyes. Her inner ugliness bites at him. His face tightens. Suddenly he is older, worn. "Honey," she says, this time in her most saccharin and calculating tone. She hates herself for this. Calling him "honey" makes her sound like her mother. Calling him "honey" makes her feel like a liar.

Julie is quiet. She watches Ethan take a small bottle of water from the refrigerator. She can't help but be amused by his white pajamas. Ethan begins sorting the mail on the counter. Head down, his body turned sideways. He can't look at her, can he?

She feels her nose spreading across her face. This is just as her mother warned. Julie envisions her mother lifting yet another dry turkey sandwich to her mouth, "The older you get the more bulbous your nose becomes."

"I think that old lady died," Julie points to the window.

"It's getting late," Ethan says without glancing up. "Why don't you just come to bed, Tiny?"

Julie stares at her husband's small hands with their crooked fingers; small hands that will one day, without a doubt, be riddled with arthritis. Yet as she watches him lift the bottle of water to his mouth she is aware that these same hands are the very hands she fell in love with. In the dark, at the movies, his buttered fingers locked with hers. "If this is the love he's offering me, I can do this," she whispered to herself then.

"Tiny?" he asks again.

"I really think she died, Ethan."

"Tiny, please come to bed." His voice barely perceptible.

"I'll be there in a minute," she says and walks over to the peaches. "I want to make these for Teddy." She lifts the small bag of peaches off the counter and opens them to show Ethan.

"That's nice," he says, shaking his head and leaving the room.

Julie doesn't mind him. She returns to the sink, washes her hands, begins peeling the peaches. She can't explain why she thinks the old lady is dead, but there is something. Something about the way the light casts itself on that single bare plate. Julie knows things about her neighbor. She's an old woman with yellow toile in her kitchen. An old woman alone, white hair, dated pictures. An old woman who had money, but never wealth. An old woman longing to die.

Julie plops the peaches into boiling water one by one. *Ethan can't conceive of someone wanting to die, but Ethan is normal.* Julie lights another cigarette. Her chest burns. She'll have a cough tomorrow.

Within minutes the peaches are tender. Julie removes them from the pot, allows them to cool a bit before blending. In the meantime she searches her kitchen cabinets for a specific bowl, a small china bowl her father sent just after Teddy's birth. When she finds it she holds it by its rim for a second or two before removing it. He hasn't even seen his grandson.

The peaches are perfect, chunky, just the right texture for a one-year-old. Julie stops the blender, eases the purée out with a spatula, wipes the counter, rinses the pot, covers the bowl with plastic wrap and puts Teddy's peaches in the refrigerator.

Tomorrow she'll proudly report this to Dr. Edelman: peaches and a Knicks game. Julie walks toward the bedroom. She feels silly but Dr. Edelman will encourage her. It shouldn't always be about what Julie can't do, the spoon, the bath. The peaches are important too. All these little deeds are tiny triumphs, shameless victories.

Even without her doctor's reassurance, Julie accepts that these are what she must accomplish. These are the infinitesimally small steps she must take in order to claim her life.

NINE

Ethan is sleeping. Streetlight creeps in through the sides of the blackout shades. Julie takes off her pants and slips into bed. Her husband's low-pitched breath lingers heavy in the air, impenetrable. She watches his eyelids flicker.

She hopes Ethan's dreams are good dreams, a simple walk in the park, an easy night at the movies. She worries about scarring, how she has scarred him. Julie wanted, still wants to spare him. If it's true that trust is what makes a man vulnerable, then loving her will destroy him.

Loving her will destroy both of them, bit by bit, little by little.

"I don't want you to hate me," she said the night Ethan proposed.

"Hate you? How could I ever hate you?"

She studies Ethan's face, easy in sleep. How can she possibly be offended by his hesitation? She must touch him, put her hand on his shoulder, press her lips into his back. It is up to her to let him know that she's strong enough to be wanted again.

Julie leans back into her pillow, her mouth dry from smoke. *But why do I have to be the one to initiate everything? You are going to fail. You can't help but fail.* "Stop," she whispers.

She opens her eyes and focuses on the Venetian armoire at the other end of the room. She has to be the one to fix this marriage because she's the one who broke it in the first place. What do you want, little guy? Remember that?

Again that instant plays out in her head. Teddy's lips were so soft, so minute, so easy to swallow. She stuck her tongue into her son's mouth just to feel what it would be like to be one with him again. She missed that, being one with him. His tongue was moist and foolish against her own. Innocent to the first kiss she was stealing from him. Innocent to all that she would continue to steal.

Julie lifts herself off the bed and walks back into the hall. Night-lights. Tears begin to fill her eyes. All of her silly precautions. She wanders into the living room, looking for her father. He smiles at her, far away in time, blameless.

It all seems so obvious to her now, his easiness in the photograph. "You always knew you'd leave," she says out loud as she holds him in her hands. Her father close by yet nowhere she can call. He is nothing more than a memory, she reminds herself again. Nothing more than the feelings evoked by an old Springsteen song.

Damn him. She looks around her apartment at all her pretty things. Her father cheated her. And he'd laugh if he saw her as she is right now. Holding his picture. Angry around the corners of her eyes, slowly aging.

Julie sits on the living-room window seat. Snowflakes float down from a darkened sky. This is when she misses him the most. In the winter, in the cold, wearing a turtleneck, a knotty sweater. Beneath these layers, she safely misses him.

"Sweetheart, look out the window." Julie hears his gentle voice, feels his enormous hand stroke the back of her head. "Count the snowflakes and then you'll know how much I love you."

Tonight's snow seems thin, wet. Julie stands, straightening her back with certainty. If only better posture could reduce the damage of that specific memory. It's past two in the morning. *It's time,* she thinks, walking back down the hall, *it's time to go to sleep.*

Julie checks on Teddy. She raises the light cotton blanket up to his shoulders. Cold has always been a fear of hers. Not heat. Heat she can survive. But a creeping freeze seems impossible. Julie places the palm of her hand over the top of Teddy's round head. His hair is growing in darker. His head becoming harder. But each of his little breaths still holds goodness. She hasn't stolen it all. Not yet.

Dr. Edelman insists that kissing Teddy the way Julie had that morning was normal. That it is, in fact, hormonal to be attracted to your child when first born, especially when breastfeeding. That she isn't guilty. That she hasn't and won't cross the boundaries of acceptable behavior.

Julie runs her finger down the slope of her son's nose. His nostrils widen from her touch, his body squirms. Still, even with Dr. Edelman's reassurance Julie can't fathom how she will meet the expectations. Good wife, reliable daughter. Devoted sister, nurturing mother.

Julie climbs into bed. The sheets and blanket are snug, cozy. She presses her head into the pillow. The fear of troubled sleep keeps her awake. Julie glances around the dimly lit room. Is this how she will spend the remainder of her life, battling sleep in this unforgiving room?

Maybe they should move into a different neighborhood, an apartment in Carnegie Hill, more amenities, more full-time mothers like herself. Maybe a loft in Tribeca, white walls, space. Just last weekend she and Ethan looked at houses in the suburbs. There was that one nice one, a white center hall Colonial, white with green shutters.

"Ethan." She touches his arm. He moves only slightly. "Eth," she asks again.

"Tine?"

He rolls toward her. "I'm sorry to wake you. I just wanted you to know it's snowing."

Ethan lifts himself up onto his elbow and looks at her.

"The snow made me think of that pretty house we saw."

His sleepy eyes smile.

Julie wants to be this for him: A woman in lilac with a thick long braid and a tennis racket. Julie moves closer. He will protect me, she thinks. Ethan is a different man than her father.

"Where the fuck is she, Ron? Where are you hiding her?"

"What are you talking about, Harriet? Hiding who?"

"Whoever the little slut is you're fucking."

Julie remembers looking at her mother and then quickly looking away. Her mother's eyes were frantic, her own guilty.

"Harriet." Her father's voice hung long and heavy in the cool winter night.

"Julie?" her brother asked.

Julie covered David's eyes with her hands. Moving cars screeched to a halt. There was lots of noise, people running, people shouting. But in Julie's head it all went quiet as she watched her mother run into the traffic on Forty-Second Street.

"What are you doing?" her father had hollered as he grabbed at her. Harriet only got a foot or two off the sidewalk before she fell.

"What the fuck do you think I'm doing, Ron? I'm trying to kill myself, Ron. I hate you. You fucking ruined my life. Look at me. You fucking ruined me."

Julie remembers her mother rocking back and forth, knees curled into her chest, mascara running down her face. "Where is she?" her mother asked again, her voice growing softer and softer as she continued to rock.

Julie also remembers that it took her father two times to get her mother up off the ground. The first time she was able to pull away, but the second time he managed to drag her up to her feet. Then, as if nothing happened, the four of them continued walking toward the theater. Their mother's heels high, her step uneven. A large wet spot stained the back of her suede coat.

"Look, Mommy peed in her pants," David said as they trailed behind. How old was he then, five, six?

Ethan extends his arm, opening himself to her. This is what Julie has of the world. This is it. The little boy asleep in the next room and this foolish man still brave enough to love her. Julie moves her body closer. She has no other alternative. She must force herself to believe that Ethan won't do the things she had seen her father do.

Julie pictures her father as he was at the Knicks game. Maybe he'll marry the woman he was with. Maybe he'll have a baby with her. She sees her, she's two-ish his new daughter, two years old, hair in bunches, white tights. The little girl is gripping her father's big steady hand. He stops and buys her an ice-cream cone. He holds the cone for her, wipes away the white cream with his thumb as it gathers on her lips. Her name, this time, Julie imagines, is Daisy.

The softness of Ethan's pajama top feels like a safe place to rest. Ethan takes Julie's hand in his own; he lifts her shirt up past her elbow and then looks to her for permission. Julie nods. He moves his thumb over her wrist, then stops. "They're getting better," he says, drawing her in close.

Memories float in and out of Julie's head. Who taught her to carve a pumpkin, play patty-cake, make angels in the snow? Who closed which door? Who used what fingers? Who took deep breaths? Who took small ones? Did it hurt? Did she yell? Did she whisper? Is she lying?

Sometimes, Julie knows that Ethan still thinks she is capable of being all the things he wants her to be. Tonight, as he holds her in his arms real tight, she can almost find a way to believe him.

TEN

Julie wakes, walks into the bathroom. Last night was a start. Ethan touched her. She catches herself. What she sees in the mirror is something she must accept. Paler, heavier, there is no changing who she is or any of what happened.

There are still choices. She can run away and start over. A suitcase. A few grand. A farm town. Cows, sheep, anonymity. She can be a ticket taker at a small theater in Iowa. A librarian up in Poughkeepsie. No family. No responsibility. Nothing to owe. But still her father will be with her. No matter where she goes. Always his eyes will shine through her, haunting her this way.

She shares his chin too, even his mouth. Naked, her shoulders are more narrow. Her chest and torso long like her mother's. Her legs a mixture. Their feet the same. Julie stops by the living-room window. There is no snow on the ground and the sun is rising.

Julie enters the darkened kitchen. She can hear Georgie's shower running. Good, she has five, ten minutes until she has to hand her kitchen over. Julie opens the refrigerator. "Happy birthday," she says as she reaches for the peaches.

This is who she is. Another young woman in a T-shirt and sweats. Another mother waiting for her day to begin. There is a baby to feed. A husband to shuffle off to work. Errands to run. Julie fills a small glass with water and opens her medicine. It's okay, she thinks and swallows, everything is okay.

It is 1997, almost the end of 1997. Teddy Davis sits in his high chair, watching *Sesame Street*. Warm peaches are being spooned into his mouth by his mother. He claps his hands.

This is happiness, his mother thinks. A single tear slowly rolls down her face. Sometimes, when she's really brave, she lets herself remember. Once she loved Big Bird too.

Julie dreams.

"We'd like two grilled cheese sandwiches," she tells the waiter a few years from now. "Two grilled cheeses and two black-and-white shakes." They eat together. Julie goes bite for bite with her son. Another boy chattering away about baseball cards. Another young man with a future.

Through the window her father sees her, sitting across from a boy with shaggy hair. There she is, sipping from her straw, smiling. She is wearing a white T-shirt and jeans. Her arms are long, lean. Her neck straight. He stares for a minute. Then a minute longer.

She is someone's wife. Someone's mother. He takes a step back as she turns her head in his direction. He combs his fingers through his grayish hair. Is it him she needs?

He wants to walk in, pick up the check, say he's sorry.

No, it's the waiter. She points toward the counter. It's something for the boy. A doughnut? The boy looks through the window and past him. The boy has his eyes.

The man waits a minute longer. He continues watching and swears he can hear his daughter giggling. He hates her for this. For not sensing his presence. For moving on. For being able to laugh. He takes one last look. Still, he can't help but find her beautiful.

Julie turns her head back toward the television, blinks her eyes, forces his well-known shadow to fade. Teddy paws her shoulder. His mouth is open in anticipation. His eyes echo of need. She dips a small spoon into the bowl and lifts it toward his mouth. "Forgive me," she whispers, tracing her finger across his brow. Life has taught her to love this way.

"Hey," Ethan says as he walks into the kitchen. He bends over and gives Julie a kiss on her cheek, then walks around the table to his son. Julie watches her husband brush the palm of his hand down the back of their son's head.

She realizes just then that Ethan's small hands are deceiving. He is a force of nature, a man who pounds into things, a German shepherd masquerading as a lap dog. And in the end, this is probably what she loves most about him, his spirit. Julie stirs her bowl of peaches. His spirit and his innocence.

Teddy reaches. "Da Da," the little boy says, motioning toward his father. Ethan smiles and lifts his son out of the chair. "Happy Birthday, champion." He turns toward his wife still smiling.

Yes, she knows. He is happy about Teddy's birthday, about her peaches, about all of it.

"What are you doing today, hon?" He is bouncing Teddy in his arms.

"Just doctors, Dr. Edelman, the gyno."

"Great," he says as he puts Teddy back in the high chair, "and what about your mom?"

"I'm not sure I'm ready to see her like that."

"I understand," he says, opening the morning paper.

Their days before the accident began just this way. Each day the *Times* and the *Post* are delivered to the door. Each day there is a gossip page, a sports page. Each day the stock market goes up or down. Each day people are going and growing and doing things. In two or three minutes Ethan will leave. Julie pictures her husband walking down the street. Even in a suit Ethan still looks like a boy. How much different is he really than Will from upstairs?

And yes, Julie reassures herself. Part of her is still like that Charlotte, holding her boyfriend's hand and following him down the street. Part of her is still young enough to believe in a night at the Beacon. Julie turns her head. She hadn't heard Ethan's question.

"What do you want to do for dinner?"

Georgie walks out of her bedroom.

"Good morning, Mister…" She opens the freezer and removes a bag of coffee. She turns and faces the table, "and Mrs." Julie swears Georgie just said "Mrs." with a cool tone, a knowing smile. But who cares? It's silly.

It's silly for her to care how Georgie addresses her. Sillier still for her to resent Georgie's pressed uniform, her neat white slippers, her ironed tights. Julie knows it's not about the woman's appearance. It's rather nice that she wears her hair pinned back, small gold balls in her ears. But right or wrong, Julie can't help herself. Every time that woman comes out of her room, "Fresh coffee, Mr. Ethan?"

Ethan looks at Julie and then at Georgie. By offering her husband coffee Georgie reminds both of them that it is her grace and her grace alone that is allowing Julie this moment to pretend.

"No thanks," he answers, pushing back his chair. He is sparing his wife the details of Georgie's domesticity. A rich cup of coffee, an evenly toasted bialy. Julie appreciates this kindness. Somehow he knows she needs to, whether it's pretending or not, pretend a little longer.

It's Julie's day. Julie's day to feel powerful in the kitchen. But it doesn't matter. Peaches or no peaches, everybody in the room understands that she is far from whole.

This is why for the past few mornings Julie's chosen to stay in bed. From there she only has to hear the sound of oranges being squeezed. After her first morning back home she decided it was better not to actually see it. She didn't have to witness Georgie serving her husband in the ways she was supposed to. Cutting a nice rounded orange down the middle. Squeezing it, straining the pulp, all the while holding Teddy in her arms. A complete breakfast is as simple as paying a salary. A complete life for Ethan could be bought for five hundred dollars a week. And he could pay less. Five hundred is a lot.

In bed, there is darkness. Julie can curl herself up into a ball. Safely wait for Ethan to leave, for her own day to begin. And it should begin slowly. She learned this while she was away. She needs to pace herself.

Away, she had found a certain serenity. The hospital had all those things from the movies. Open fields covered with snow. Neatly shoveled paths. It must be gorgeous here in the spring, Julie thought to herself as she stared out of the window. From her hospital bed she was able to see a small-town church in the distance. She thought of a Chekhov story she had read in college: peasants walking across long open fields, faith.

Julie looks into the foyer and watches as Ethan buttons his overcoat. Part of her wanted to stay up in Connecticut. Sometimes, from beneath the covers of that bed, she fantasized about remaining there long enough to become a person. Winter, spring, summer, fall. She pictured herself leaner, stronger. She didn't want to leave until she was able to make a pot of coffee, give her baby a bath, fuck.

"I'll take care of dinner," Julie says, standing up from her chair.

"Really?" A tentative, curious optimism coats Ethan's face. "You don't have to feel any pressure or anything. We can go out."

"No, I want to. I do. I really want to make Teddy a birthday dinner."

"That's nice," he says. His voice lost for a second, head down, hand fumbling through his pocket in search of a glove. But they made her leave. One month later and she was "okay" to leave.

Julie turns to check on Teddy. No worry, *Sesame Street*'s holding him content and Georgie's back there lurking around. Julie's stomach feels its familiar unease. She takes a few steps and opens the front door for Ethan.

"You are going to do great," the nurse said as she helped Julie put her few belongings into a bag. But Julie wasn't sure. She felt at ease in the hospital. Everyone's role was determined. There were the doctors, the nurses. People to decide what you should eat, people to cook the meal, people to serve it. There were scheduled times, activity time, talk time, rest time.

At the hospital Julie was certain of her position. She was the patient, almost the same uniform as a doctor but not quite. She felt comfortable among her rank. For them, taking a nap in the morning was following orders.

"So good-bye," Ethan says.

Julie looks at him, both gloves in his left hand, his briefcase in his right, a black knit cap on his head. It's the first time they are standing together at the front door since that day. She wants to go over and kiss him, but she feels awkward, and somewhat defeated. It was here that she deceived him. Right in this spot she held their boy in her arm and waved good-bye, full of we love you, Daddy, and have a nice day.

In the hospital Julie was able to relinquish much of her regret. But out here in the real world regret swarms around her. She watches Ethan press for the elevator.

He brought her a brand-new outfit to wear home, a maroon sweater, tan wool pants, black leather shoes. Everything came gift-wrapped in a big box from Saks Fifth Avenue. Ethan's intention, Julie felt when she saw the clothes, was to make the day a celebration of sorts. Mommy was coming home.

So she gladly slipped on the sweater, pulled up the pants. The clothes felt comfortable, smooth. They were easy, nothing was too tight. Somehow Ethan had picked the right size. Probably a helpful salesgirl. "How lucky your wife is."

But when Julie opened the shoebox she wanted to cry. She didn't wear loafers. Her mother wore loafers but she didn't wear loafers. What was Ethan trying to tell her after all? She put them on anyway. They were narrow, restricting. Her step felt uneasy as she moved around the room. Too much newness pressing against her flesh. Too much, already, of his tidy expectation.

You are going to fail. You can't help but fail. Julie somehow found it in herself to ignore that doubting voice. She couldn't stay there. She had a husband, a son. Moving forward was the tacit understanding. So Julie went home. Loafers and all, she followed her husband. Through the hospital's revolving door and into the light of another expectant morning.

Julie is still waiting with Ethan for the elevator. The navy sweats that she is wearing were his once, old fraternity sweatpants. She remembers he was playing football on the quad the first time they saw each other. She was heading back to her dorm room, books tucked under her right arm.

"Hey," he said, tossing the football back and forth between his hands as he walked toward her. Six feet tall, full of confidence and student loans.

"Your eyes are some kind of blue." She blushed.

The elevator rumbles to a stop and the doors open. Ethan turns to her one last time before entering. Her slight smile offers only a hint of her apology.

ELEVEN

She could be anyone. Outside, daylight presses against her cheeks. Her dark hair is tied back, bunched. She is wearing jeans, the same leather jacket. Her sneakers, once white, are grayish. Running shoes. Narrow and unlaced. She will spend this day alone. She will do some of the things she has to do. She will go to Dr. Edelman's at noon, cross her legs, lean into the cool leather of the Eames chair. She will face her new doctor, try to look her in the eyes, try to talk. And they will talk, about her medicine, about how she's feeling. Okay. She is okay.

But first she has her yearly at the gyno's. She scheduled this check-up so many months ago and now, all of a sudden, the day is here. One year.

Julie pushes open the heavy mahogany door to Dr. Salzman's office. She is going to get the chance to thank the doctor again and so what? If he wants to talk to her about what happened she'll talk to him about it. The important thing for her to remember is that "what happened" is precisely that, something that happened. A period of her life that's behind her. Today is about Teddy's birthday and a Pap smear.

Julie walks over to the front desk. She is in luck, a new receptionist. This woman doesn't know Julie, doesn't even know her name, definitely doesn't know her history.

"Sure," Julie answers. She is more than happy to review her file and yes all the information is still appropriate, her phone number, her birth date, her insurance, "Still Oxford?"

"Still Oxford."

Too bad for Oxford. Julie takes a seat in the waiting room. She flips through a few magazines, *Parents* and *Parenting, Baby.* She decides on *People*, never any pressure with *People*. Every once in a while she looks up from what she's reading and glances at the other women in the waiting room.

She wonders who's happily married, where each of them live. She creates worlds for them. The WASP sitting across the room from her, the mother with the blonde-headed girl next to her is from Greenwich. Greenwich or New Canaan. They have a nice house out there, drove into the city for a checkup and to spend the day. Maybe lunch at the Plaza, a little shopping at Bergdorf's, a haircut.

Julie pegs the older woman sitting just to her right as a professional. Some big-time lawyer or broker. A successful woman with a career as hearty as her briefcase. But look at her, with all that homework she forgot to have a kid. She'll get one though, in-vitro's pretty much a no-brainer these days.

The woman walking into the office right now intrigues Julie most. The woman drops her jacket on an unoccupied chair, sashays over to the receptionist, all put together, wool skirt, tight cashmere sweater, pumps. Julie can't even imagine, eight, nine months pregnant, look at that belly, the middle of winter and Manolo Blahnik pumps?

Julie glances at the clock, outside at the bare trees. She waits patiently for the nurse to announce her turn. But when she is announced, when she finally hears the heavyset receptionist call out, "Julie Davis," Julie doesn't move. Instead she looks around the room. First at the woman holding her file, then at the other women in the waiting room. She does this partially for reassurance, for permission to stand and enter. She wants them to give her a signal of some sort, a bit of encouragement.

But mostly she doesn't move because she's still surprised. Surprised to find herself here. "Mrs. Julie Davis." Julie checks her hands, her feet. She looks up and away again. This is who she is, "Mrs. Julie Davis." It's time, she thinks, and stands.

In the examining room Julie stares at the medical table. At the neatly organized syringes, at the box of rubber gloves, a tube of lubricant. She unfolds the flimsy paper robe, looks at it intently for a second or two, not sure if it should be opened to the back or to the front. At the hospital she wore a cloth robe or hospital pajamas. At the hospital she never saw a syringe, or a box of rubber gloves, or any kind of lubricant.

The nurse enters. She puts down the file and looks at Julie. These two know each other in a sense. This nurse's name is Barbara. She's the nurse who rubbed jelly on Julie's stomach, taught her how to make out Teddy's heartbeat. "Sorry to hear you've had such a hard time."

Julie tries to smile but keeps her lips closed.

Barbara waits a second, then gestures toward the scale. As she readjusts the balance Julie turns her head away. She knows now not to look; if she doesn't see the number she won't be able to define herself by the number. *Not in a number.* But Barbara reveals it, "One hundred and twenty," she says as she slides the weight back to zero.

One hundred and twenty pounds is heavier than Julie wants to be. Heavier than she has ever been, other than when she was pregnant. Heavier than high school, heavier than college, heavier than the day she married Ethan.

"Perfectly average." Barbara records Julie's weight in her chart. Julie has become this somehow, average, a girl of average weight. "See you in a minute, hon." Barbara closes the door. Julie can reach for another magazine, *Good Housekeeping, Redbook*. Although she decides, instead, to lie down.

Alone, on her back in the examining room, the fluorescent bulb buzzes. Julie stares up at it. It doesn't matter, she reminds herself, everyone has a history, some story or another. And lots of people weigh more than one hundred and twenty pounds.

Julie decides right then that if she has to beg she will. She'll beg Dr. Salzman to tell her the truth. She wants to know how it looks down there. If she's old, stretched? She's been wondering about this lately. The markings time has left on her.

As usual Dr. Salzman gives two quick knocks before he enters. Julie sits up, her hands folded, legs crossed. He walks through the door, always neat and tidy, always a fast and efficient smile. Today, though, it's a little different. "Hey, Julie." Today he starts his exam by giving her a hug.

Julie is on her back, staring at the ceiling again. Dr. Salzman presses his fingers into her left breast. Each time he does this her nipple becomes more enlarged, more erect. He checks her right one and the same thing happens. Now Julie is lying on her back with two erect nipples. "Looks good," he says, directing his attentions downward.

She wants to apologize for not being waxed. She should have gone and gotten waxed at the Korean place on Columbus or at least trimmed herself. But other than washing, she hasn't even thought about it, touching it, grooming. How embarrassing, with all the pussies he sees she's probably…"I'm sorry I'm so hairy." Julie expresses this regret with a hint of laughter in her voice. He chuckles. Barbara does too, albeit tentatively.

Dr. Salzman puts Julie's left foot into a stirrup, then her right. He opens her knees. "I'm going to stick the speculum in. You ready?"

Julie nods. He sticks the tool in. She can feel it opening wider, can feel him inside her, scraping around. After Dr. Salzman finishes collecting all that he needs to collect from her, he rubs what he's taken against a smooth piece of glass. Again, she finds herself trying to be funny because she has to say something about it, doesn't she?

"The only positive is with all that blood loss I skipped my period." Julie's trying to let the air out of the room. Why not say the unsaid? After all, look at her; her back is already up against the table. She could wear this paper robe upside down for all it mattered. Any which way her scars are exposed. Unless there's some sort of thing she doesn't know about, some way to make a paper robe grow sleeves.

But neither the doctor nor the nurse laugh this time. Dr. Salzman looks up at her from the stool he is seated on. His head still between her legs. "Julie, when was the last time you had your period?" *Is he being serious?* She wants to push back, tries to push back, but the thing's in her. She stills.

"I don't know," she says, trying to calculate. They had sex the night before she went to the hospital, that's clear. She felt better as soon as she got home from the party. Ethan paid the sitter, unzipped her dress, began by kissing the back of her neck. She went to the hospital the next day, stayed there for a few weeks. She's been home for three days. "I really don't know, a month ago, a month and a half."

Dr. Salzman eases the clamp out and stands, "Okay, last thing and your exam will be over." Barbara applies lubricant to his pointer finger. He rolls Julie onto her side, sticks his finger into her ass, moves it around. "Terrific," he says as he pulls out. "Why don't you go into the bathroom and leave me your urine. Then meet me in my office."

In the bathroom Julie takes one of the small paper cups that say Meridian Labs. She covers the toilet seat with a bit of toilet paper on each side. She squats at first and then decides to sit.

She pees into the paper cup and rests it to the right of the faucet. Her urine is too yellow. She must drink more water, even if it makes her feel fat. Look how dark, so dehydrated. She wipes herself, stands, washes her hands.

In this mirror her eyes are red, redder than they had been earlier in the morning, her face flushed. She looks at her urine in the cup, at the toilet seat, at the bathroom door. She yells at him then. Silently, without uttering a word, she yells at Ethan for inhabiting her.

Julie is waiting for Dr. Salzman. There are things she wants to do today. She wants to make chicken cutlets. Today is her son's first birthday. She wants to bake him a cake. She passes the time by looking at the pictures on Dr. Salzman's desk. He has four children, two girls, two boys. He has a beautiful wife, a dead ringer for Sharon Stone, same wide smile, also blonde. In this picture they are outside a house, probably their country home, some horsy place upstate. She must ride, the wife. An equestrian, the tall boots, the riding pants, the crop.

The doctor pats Julie's shoulder with his hand and then walks across his office to his desk. He helped her when she was pregnant with Teddy, helped her with the eating, talked to her, insisted she do silly little things like take the time to breathe. He sits down. The wall behind him is covered with medical diplomas, Northwestern, NYU.

He fingers a small rubber ball on his desk. He presses the blue ball into the palm of his hand. It loses its shape, contracts. He lets go and the ball opens itself up to him. Julie watches him do this several times before speaking.

"When?" she finally asks. He pushes the ball to the side and looks at her.

"August. First week in August." His response is followed by silence.

"August," Julie's voice begins to break, "August is hot."

Dr. Salzman comes over and sits down in the chair next to her. The chair reserved for the husband. The husband who comes to hold his wife's hand, to celebrate their good news, their good fortune. Ethan had been that man once.

"Are you sure?"

The doctor nods.

Julie knows now that it can never be. That she will never be sixteen again, a virgin. She will never have the pink little pussy she was hoping for. Tight and compact. She is certain Dr. Salzman is thinking this too, that there is nothing left of her that's pure.

"Do you want me to call Ethan?"

"No thanks," she says as she stands. He asks her to wait and writes his home number on the back of his business card. "I'll handle this any way you want," he offers.

Julie is anyone. Any other woman with a life inside of her. Here she goes walking up Madison Avenue. She ignores the smartly dressed mannequins in the window of Valentino, pulls her cap down around her ears and keeps moving, past Fred Leighton Jewelers, where tiaras glisten on top of faceless heads, past the gift shop where little Santa men dance in the store window.

She turns away from the mother racing to the park with her baby carriage, away from the lady with the Yorkie, away from the elderly woman in blue earmuffs. Julie's pace quickens then slows. Her expression as dead and cool as the winter air.

TWELVE

It was early winter the first time her father missed coming home. Julie remembers her mother buried beneath a quilted yellow bedspread, waiting. He came back to them through the garage door, shaggy black hair framing his face, his silk shirt unbuttoned, mounds of dark chest hair. He carried the newspaper in one hand, his briefcase in the other.

Everything about him smelled new, like the leather interior of his new car. "Morning, flower," he said as he kissed Julie on top of her head. "Hey, big guy," he said to David, same cheery voice, same wet kiss. Two, three days away. He went over to the fridge, opened it, poured himself a glass of orange juice. How was he able to come home smiling like that?

Julie passes through the revolving door of her mother's apartment building. Her mother had thought that living in the city would placate Ron. She sold their house and moved him to Park Avenue. But she had underestimated his wants. How could she have allowed herself to believe, even for a second, that a half-bottle of Chianti and a thin-crust pizza would appease him?

It was only a matter of months until Ron fell prey to temptation. In New York City, where all men are created equal, all men are free.

Julie shakes her head. The dimness of the lobby is blinding. She turns in what she knows is the direction of the concierge and waves. Here, she can be this for her mother, the pretty daughter coming to visit.

She heads toward the elevator, her step unsure on the thick red carpeting. She checks her watch. She can stay ten, twenty minutes at the most before she must leave for Dr. Edelman's. But twenty minutes is better than nothing. At least she's doing the right thing. She has to visit her mother. How do you not visit your mother?

Julie presses for the elevator. The lobby of her mother's building is really rich-looking. Although it's nicer when there isn't this carpeting. Julie digs her toe into the ground. When the warm weather comes, this carpet will be rolled up and put into storage. The cool white slabs of marble that lie beneath it will have the chance to breathe again.

Julie presses for a second time. By then, she looks around. A lot can happen by then. The doors open. She asks to be taken to the third floor, "Three, please." She puts her head down, hoping the elevator attendant won't talk to her. But it doesn't work. "You Mrs. Patamkin's daughter?"

"Yes." Julie looks up and smiles.

It's funny to hear her mother referred to as Mrs.

"Pretty lady, Mrs. Patamkin."

Julie nods. "What's your name?"

This asking of names started in the hospital, so many different people walking in and out of her room. She thought if she could thank each one personally they might know how much she appreciated all that they did for her. Their name and maybe another detail, a boyfriend, a kid, a husband.

Her interest didn't only apply to the doctors and nurses. She especially cared who brought her meals, who took away her garbage.

"Pablo, ma'am."

"Nice to meet you, Pablo." Julie isn't being insincere when she says this. It *is* nice to meet him and she *will* make an effort to remember his name. But in truth, by the end of the day, who's she kidding, by the time she gets off of the elevator his name will have vanished.

"Thanks," she says, stepping out on three. Julie turns to the left, *311, 313*. She can feel his eyes following her. He'll go away. *315, 319*. Julie rings the bell to her mother's apartment and waits.

Harriet opens the door. As soon as Julie sees her she realizes she shouldn't have come. Her mother's face is bloated, the corners of her mouth stained, her eyes swollen. There are staples by her ears and just below her hairline. "Hi, Ma," Julie says, trying to act as if her mother's appearance is normal.

She follows her mother into the apartment and down the hall. All their shared memories have been crammed into this prime bit of Park Avenue real estate. The faux-Regency chairs they bought on a trip to France in '88. The baby grand piano that no one but David ever played. "I'm so happy you're here," Harriet says, motioning Julie into the living room.

Her father's pictures are still everywhere, in jeweled frames collected over the years. Julie hates him now for being stuck there between them. She even wonders, as she passes a matching set of framed collages, how she might possibly edit him out while still salvaging the photographs.

"You look good, Ma."

"Never mind that. Sit down, honey." Julie sits on the corner of the cream sofa. A leafy-colored throw rests at the other end.

There is a familiar crystal bowl filled with sugar-free jelly candies in the center of the coffee table. A larger version of the same bowl is placed just to its left. The larger bowl overflowing with dried rose petals.

The room is centered around this mother-of-pearl coffee table, which is actually too large for the space that it finds itself in, but it works well enough. Harriet's acceptably old, but not antique, Aubusson carpet brings the room together and of course there is her mildly unattractive but not dreadful Larry Rivers up on the wall.

Harriet walks over to a blackened television. She wears flat shoes these days. Smooth calfskin loafers that she buys two pairs at a time. "You won't believe this," she says slowly, enunciating each syllable.

It's almost, Julie thinks to herself as she continues to listen, it's almost as if her mother's trying to stall. Stall her thoughts until she's able to understand them or at least contain them. Julie doesn't fault her mother. There is always the hope that if you hold things together long enough you might prevent them from crumbling around you.

"You won't believe this." Harriet's voice as deliberate as ever. She presses Play. The television screen lights and focuses. There is the boardwalk, the same boardwalk of Julie's childhood. A motionless Ferris wheel is in the background, just behind what is now an abandoned arcade.

Julie had begged her mother point-blank not to have them followed. But there they are, same blonde he was with last night. There she is again, sitting on his lap, laughing. The clarity of the picture is perfect. Ron's holding a cone to her mouth, how he loves to feed.

Asbury Park is empty this time of year, Julie thinks as she watches the footage. Still this woman, this young lady not much older than herself, must find her father terribly romantic. There they are laughing again. How wonderful, the Jersey shore in December.

Harriet pauses, rewinds, pauses. The twenty-four-inch screen plays out all of what it's holding. But it isn't enough. It can never be enough. Harriet creeps closer to the television. She kneels inches from the screen just where she had warned Julie and her brother never to sit if they wanted to keep their eyesight.

One lick for her, one for him. Scattered pages of newspaper dancing about their feet.

Julie watches her mother shrink before the screen. Her narrow waist is belted too tight even for her small frame. She has successfully transformed herself into another woman. A woman with a tapered nose, an erect jaw, a fine chin. Soon the staples will be removed and with time the redness will fade, the swelling will subside. The lines that had warmed the edges of what were her mother's eyes are already gone. This woman's eyes are taut. Her mouth wide. If you look happy and pretty, then you are happy and pretty.

Harriet asked the doctor to make her look awake. It appears that what bothered her the most, other than the jowls, is that she looked tired. From where Julie sits the plastic surgeon more than succeeded. This version of Harriet appears perpetually alert. So alert it seems to Julie as though her mother might bite the television.

But then there are her shoulders. Julie looks at her mother's shoulders. They give her away, curving downward, frowning from behind. They'll always do this, carry her age.

Pause, rewind, pause. "Not a very pretty girl, really, don't you think, Jule? Thirty-five, never been married, that has to say something." In the picture, the air seems crisp but the boardwalk looks abandoned, old and dirty. "Damn this tape. It's so blurry," Harriet says, too close for any perspective.

Harriet pushes herself up off the floor, walks over to the couch, and sits next to her daughter. Surprisingly, her smell is slightly sour, almost flat. Julie looks around the room. Her mother has always kept a spotless home. Look at the bookshelves, tidy and arranged, no dust. The books are mostly biographies, John F. Kennedy, Martin Luther King, Ali. All the predictable heroes for a guy like Ron.

Julie decides she needn't correct her mother about the girl's attractiveness. Why mention that she saw them? What's there to say? That not only is the girlfriend pretty but she's tall, that Dad's hair is black again, that he looks great: thin, no bloat? *He asked how you are, Ma*, can you imagine? Why even get started down that path? *I said you were doing great.* Boy, that will make her feel better, won't it?

Julie notices her father's coat hanging by the front door, still wrapped in plastic from the dry-cleaner. She studies her mother, watches as she draws the bowl of diet candy toward them. She hasn't accepted it, has she?

In his new life Ron is a man without a wife and kids, without grandkids, certainly without a camel coat. In his new life he is a man in black. He is Johnny Cash. No, he's even better than Johnny Cash.

Whatever her father is or isn't, it's certainly clear from the video that he's single. A single man in the single man's uniform. And she is young, blonde, and clearly taken in by all of it: the cold ocean air, the ancient boardwalk, his black boots.

"We should have left." Harriet lifts an orange candy to her mouth. Julie doesn't know how her mother wants her to respond. She had been asking to leave since she was a little girl.

She kept a bag packed, a light blue suitcase, an outfit for her, for David. A toothbrush, a Barbie. She was willing to run off at any time, day, night. Sure it was confusing. After all, she loved her father more than anything in the world. But she didn't like him coming home like he did that morning and all the other mornings that followed. She didn't like watching her mother spend day after day in bed with the curtains drawn tight.

Julie always believed that her mother should have taken her and David away from that house, started a new life, sheltered them. She should, at the very least, have left him before he left them. Although, as Julie can attest, it doesn't matter much who leaves who first.

"The thing is," Harriet continues as she chews her candy, "do you think we would really have been any better off if I were working behind the Lancôme counter?"

It's almost funny to Julie that this remains her mother's fear. A small garden apartment off Route 10, working behind the Lancôme counter at Macy's. "Do you?"

Julie wants to answer, "Yes." She wants to look at her mother and say, "Yes, Ma. Yes, it would have been better because we might have been happy." But Julie doesn't say anything. She knows what her mother's response to that will be. She'll say one of two things, maybe both. She'll say, "Who would have married me with two little kids?" Or she'll say, "Look around at all these pictures. We *were* happy."

Julie glances at the image in one of the small frames on the end table. Fine, if they were so happy—she looks at her brother, if we were so happy, then why is he so fucked up? There's no arguing that David's lost, still searching for a place to go home to, a scrap of something familiar.

Just one, maybe two months ago he called her collect from their old kitchen. She couldn't believe it. He drove out to their old house, rang the doorbell, explained to the new owner who he was. And the woman let him in. David was all keyed up on the phone. "The refrigerator still smells like Mom's salad dressing."

Her brother should be in college, dating girls, playing football. But instead he's a dropout living with a bunch of roommates downtown, smoking pot, writing songs, doing whatever he can to make his pain go away.

Because it happens, even if you know who the person is: their distorted view of the world, their tainted thoughts, perverted longings. Even if you've come to accept that it will never work out: that he'll never be who he promised, who you want him to be, who you need him to be.

Even if you are lucky enough to recognize any or all of these things it won't change much. Because here you are, heartbroken. Because nothing, nothing you do, nothing he does, nothing will ever stop you from loving him.

Julie has four years on her brother. That's a lot of extra time to figure things out. A lot of extra time to shape a good-bye. She also has a husband and a kid but in spite of all of that it's hard. So who's she to judge? Still, at this moment Julie wants to take her mother by the shoulders and shake her until her breath stops or at least until she admits their father is really gone.

THIRTEEN

Julie is watching her mother bake a cake. They are in the white Formica kitchen on Deer Lane. Julie helps her mother smooth the batter around the Pyrex with a long wooden spoon. She notices that her mother's eyes are swollen, probably from crying all day.

But right now her mother isn't crying. Right now her mother is opening the oven, placing their two small, evenly battered cake dishes on the top rack. Right now, even with the swollen eyes, swollen and black with mascara, she looks beautiful. And she is beautiful. At that moment, in Julie's world, there is no one more beautiful.

Julie remembers it as if it were yesterday. She and her mother were sitting at the kitchen table, waiting for the cake to finish. Julie was planning what to do with her cake decorations, rainbow sprinkles, little silver balls, jellybeans. Harriet's eyes were closed, but every so often she'd open them and comment, "That's pretty."

The house was quiet, the middle of a Saturday afternoon, David upstairs, taking a nap. It was her mother's birthday and although Harriet was there helping, it was Julie who was making this birthday cake.

She heard the sound of the garage door opening for him. She looked at her mother, eyes still closed. Then the slam of his car door. Her mother made a noise, a short, almost stunted breath. Then she sat up straight, tossed her hair, folded her hands.

He came bearing pies, four different boxes of pies. His face was dirty from not shaving, his tie undone. He rested the boxes on the kitchen table. "Hey, honey," he said, giving Harriet a kiss.

He walked round to the side of the table. "Hey, honey," he said, kissing his daughter. There he was, back in their kitchen, calling both of them "honey." He didn't apologize, didn't mention where he'd been or even that he'd been. It had become customary for him to arrive home two days after he was supposed to.

The timer rang and Harriet stood up from the chair, put on her gloves, opened the oven. "Smells good," he said as she removed the cakes.

Her mother turned. It was a slow turn. Quiet with a motionlessness Julie has, all these years later, yet to fully understand. But it was absolutely communicating something: a warning of some sort, blame maybe, rage. Whatever its specific intent may have been, her mother's unhurried turn was surely expressing something much deeper than simple disbelief.

In response her father reached into his pocket and withdrew a small box, wrapped in shiny gold paper and tied with a red velvet ribbon. "Happy birthday," he said to her mother, his hand out, offering.

Harriet put the cake pans down to cool. Good, Julie thought, her mother was finally going to say something. But instead, she tightened her apron, walked across the checkered linoleum floor, and sat down on her husband's lap. She opted to begin by untying the ribbon.

Harriet and Julie both like the black candies and hunt for them in the bowl. Their hands touch once and they catch each other's eyes. Her mother made all the wrong choices for herself. She should have stayed down in Miami, should have lived somewhere close to her parents, should have married that nice guy she was dating when she met her father. Was his name Hank, Hank Fishbaum? That's absolutely what she should have done; she should have married Hank Fishbaum. She would have made a nice doctor's wife.

The videotape clicks off and begins rewinding. "Your grandmother used to say, 'Once a man gets one foot out the door he's never coming back.'"

Julie looks down at her hands and notices how unkempt her fingernails are next to her mother's in the bowl. Her hands look dirty in comparison. Julie stops with the candy. She doesn't have much time. She has to go soon and she wants her mother to look at her again. Actually, she wants her mother to look at her again except look at her long enough to see that she's sorry. Sorry for being the younger of the two, for having even the possibility of happiness, for in the end having stolen all her dreams.

But Harriet continues hunting for the licorice candies. Her face down, her eyes focused on the bowl. Julie watches her mother's ring-less fingers sorting through the flavors. The skin on her hand is thin. Julie sees the blood pulsing within her mother's veins. That blood, Julie supposes, is all that's left.

Even her mother's voice has changed, not that there is much anyone can do to control what happens to their voice. But instead of softening with age, Harriet's mature voice has a harshness to it that it didn't have while Julie was growing up.

"Don't drop her, Ron." Back then there was a warmth to her voice. They are walking along the same boardwalk in the video, Asbury Park twenty years ago, Kohr's ice cream, Madame Marie. A flock of seagulls breeze through the sky overhead.

"Harriet, honey, how could I drop her?"

"Well, she might not be holding on tight enough, and you might forget."

"Never." The Ferris wheel in the distance is spinning red, orange, yellow, blue. David, only a baby.

Time tingles. Julie looks at her mother's face. Her skin oily, the pores on her nose are large, a few even black. Up close the area where her eyes have been pulled back is raw. Damn him for making them love him so much, Julie thinks. Damn him for having stolen so much with leisure, on his bed, in pajamas, promising forever.

"The boardwalk is not what it used to be," is the only thing Julie can think to say.

Harriet looks up at her daughter. "Nothing is ever what it used to be," she says in defeat. "Nothing."

After a little while Julie stands up to leave but her mother doesn't move. She'll probably stay here for quite some time. Watching and rewatching. Julie reaches for her coat. In essence he has cheated them both. Look at her mother with her getting-ready-to-date overhaul. What's that going to do for her? Not much, really.

"Oh, I almost forgot." Harriet disappears for a second. She returns with a book in her hands. She passes it to Julie. "This is for you, for Teddy. I was planning on coming by today but with everything." Julie takes the book from her mother's hands and without having to look knows immediately what book it is, its familiar edges rounded with time.

"Thanks, Ma." Julie stops herself just before her voice breaks.

Harriet has resumed her position on the couch and is trying to work the remote control for the video player. "Oh, that reminds me. Did you send Gloria a thank-you note?"

"A thank-you note?"

"Yes, a thank-you note. She called me and asked if you got the flowers she sent to the hospital?" Julie leans over and touches her lips to the top of her mother's head. Bloody stitches line her mother's scalp just above her forehead. "Sorry, I didn't think of it. I'll send one today." Julie's kiss is light, fast. She is scared to and won't touch her mother any longer than this one second.

On the street noise is everywhere, cars, buses, taxis. Chattering people pass by, ladies in fur coats. Julie should get moving too. If she doesn't hurry she will be late for her appointment with Dr. Edelman. But she is just so tired. She wants to sit down on the sidewalk, not move, never move. She would melt into the concrete if she could.

Dr. Edelman's office is on the ground floor of a brownstone a few blocks north from where her mother lives. Julie checks her watch, still on time. She presses the intercom. "Yes?"

"It's Julie." She waits for the buzzer and then opens the door. Cream-colored walls, dark brown carpeting, a framed Rothko poster from the Whitney. Two coats hang on the coat rack. Julie looks at the magazines and decides on nothing, not *The New Yorker*, not *Travel and Leisure*, not *Smart Money*.

She sits down, more than happy for this little bit of time to rest herself. Some day it's been. She tries to decide what she should start with: her father, her mother, Ethan. The door to Dr. Edelman's office opens. The patient walks out, takes her coat, a black shearling, and leaves.

A few minutes pass. Julie admires the red tones in the poster, looks over toward the office door then down at the brown carpeting. It's pretty clear what she should start with. She places her hand on her stomach and waits her turn. Finally the door opens. "Come in," Dr. Edelman says with a smile on her face.

FOURTEEN

Julie sticks her key into the lock and opens her front door. Teddy and Georgie are laughing when she enters. At this very moment her presence feels like an invasion. She's an intruder in her own home. Julie is reminded of this often, of how little the choice she has made to live really matters. Thankfully, Teddy waddles toward her with his arms open. "Ma Ma."

Ma Ma bends down and scoops him up. "Ooh!" Julie says, squeezing him tight. He likes this and laughs. But when she puts him back down his whole body deflates. "I'm sorry, baby. Mommy needs to rest and then she'll take you out, okay?"

She doesn't actually wait for his response because it has to be okay. "Don't worry, ma'am," Georgie says, taking Teddy's hand. "He'll be fine." Julie accepts what Georgie says at face value because she must. Julie looks at her son standing there but stops herself. Who cares if Georgie is or isn't taunting. She needs to be alone. In darkness she will feel nothing. In darkness there is only a flicker of hope and then sleep.

Julie drops her keys and glasses on top of her vanity, leaves her sneakers by the side of the bed, draws the blinds. She puts the book her mother gave her on Ethan's pillow, then pulls the covers up past her chin until they cover her eyes.

It is four o'clock when she wakes. Two hours gone. She jumps up only to rest her head on the pillow again. She is reminded. Her hand circles the skin on her stomach. How can she allow herself to become a mother again? But if she ends this pregnancy, what is she? What would that make her? What would that make her and Ethan? Julie sits, slow to throw her legs off the bed, slow to stand.

There's still time. If she pushes herself even just a little bit she can still do all the things she wanted to do today. Run over to the market, prepare dinner. She puts on her sneakers, grabs her keys. She's not going to let herself think about the baby until Ethan gets home. Today was supposed to be about her son, and she wants it to be about him.

Julie stops in the kitchen to take her afternoon dose of medicine. There is a difference already. A slight but noticeable improvement in her mood, in her ability to concentrate, to complete things. And in another month she should feel much better. Every doctor says this. Julie nods as she opens the refrigerator and grabs an Evian. In a month everything, she swallows and begins making a list for the market: two chicken breasts, a dozen eggs, breadcrumbs, everything will be different.

Julie resolves to keep dinner simple, breaded chicken and string beans. She hears Teddy and resolves that she is not going to be insecure, she's not going to argue with Georgie, not that they actually argue, but she's not going to be intimidated. Instead, what she's going to do, she instructs herself, is walk out there and take her son to the market as if she were his mother.

Julie opens the door to Teddy's bedroom. He is up on his changing table, Georgie fixing his diaper.

"I'd like to take him out," Julie says. There is an edge to her voice she can't seem to help. Georgie looks at her, "Give me a minute," and turns back to the baby.

Loving Teddy shouldn't be a defensive request and maybe it isn't. Georgie is true to her word. She hands over Teddy, helps put him in his stroller, rests a blanket over his legs.

Julie closes the door behind her and pushes Teddy back onto the landing. She looks at the small table that separates her apartment from her neighbor's, takes a second to sort through her mail. She glances at the door to the stairwell but there's no way, no way she can carry the stroller down five sets of stairs. She checks her watch. Raymond is absolutely on duty. Absolutely waiting for her behind that wall.

What should she do when she sees him? Should she say something? She could certainly thank him. That would be a nice thing to do. But again, the same problem. *How? Thanks for helping the medics with my stretcher?*

No, she can't do that. Julie looks at Teddy and begins to worry he will get overheated if she continues to stand around like this. *I spend way too much time thinking about this stuff,* she tells herself, and presses for the elevator. It doesn't matter what either of them think of me. *I don't owe them an apology or even an explanation. She is my housekeeper. He is the elevator man.*

This is good. Julie wants to buffer herself with this class distinction. It would be so much easier for her if she didn't care. She shouldn't care. Her mother wouldn't.

But when the elevator doors open the man behind the wall isn't faceless or nameless. He is the elevator attendant. His name is Raymond. He is a man with two grown children in Puerto Rico. He is the father of another little girl born here in America to a woman not his wife. He is the man who brought them all up the day Teddy came home from the hospital. He is the man who brought her down to the ambulance. *I should feel safe with him,* Julie thinks, as she steps into the elevator.

"Mrs." he says, holding the door.

It was a mistake, she reminds herself. *I was a good mother before that day. I am a good mother now.* The elevator rumbles. She should acknowledge what had happened, thank him, something. The elevator's chains clang together; it is an old mechanism that works these manual lifts. *What a horrible job.* Up and down. Up and down. Raymond stares ahead at the wall in front of him: 5, 4, 3, 2, and then the doors open.

Mrs. Julie Davis, half owner of apartment 5B, is free to walk out of the elevator, out of the building. She can bring her baby to the street, hail a cab. She can take him with her. Together they can run away from this life. And what Julie knows now, that she hadn't grasped before, is that Raymond won't say anything. Won't even make a peep. Because Raymond is the elevator man. Because it is his job to carry people up and down without question.

Julie buttons her coat under the building's awning, places her glasses on the rim of her nose, feels for her wallet. She has her baby, his milk, a change of diapers. She needs two chicken breasts, breadcrumbs, cake mix, olive oil. No, she has oil. She needs two, no three potatoes and a small bag of string beans. She has forgotten the list but it shouldn't stop her. It's four or five things and then she can go home. She repeats this to herself and moves forward.

It is darkish out now but these early winter nights have to end sooner or later. It will be better then, she hopes. When the days are longer, when there is more light, more time to rely on.

You can see her now, stopping at the corner. There she is waiting for the light to change. She lifts the hood of the stroller and coos at her son. She itches a spot on the back of her head. *I am a good mother.*

This is the third time that she tells herself this. "I am a good mother," she mumbles, crossing the street and heading toward Broadway. She's planning on going to Fairway for fresh produce. Citarella for fresh poultry. She breastfed this baby, loved him. She was the one who dreamt him, who wanted him, who believed.

There are certain things Julie understands about herself that she didn't then. Not all of what she did, most of it actually, hadn't been her fault. She was depressed. Not, *oh I'm so depressed I can't get those shoes in my size* depressed, but depressed depressed. And they are different, these two things.

Dr. Edelman has been teaching her about it. "Depression is a condition like asthma." The antidepressant she's taking compensates for some chemical in the brain. Something or another that Julie simply "doesn't have enough of."

The problem is, just like asthma, much of how Julie's feeling on any given day is beyond her control. The symptoms can happen at any time, the tiredness, the overwhelming sorrow, the endless sense of loss. The emotions are both gradual and immediate.

It feels to Julie as if it lurks from behind, meshing itself within her memory. It reminds her again and again that there is no growing old gracefully, no love that will last forever. It insists that all of the people she loves, including her son, will leave her. It has determined that she amount to little more than another woman walking down the street in a dated fur coat, nothing but another broad the world has spit out.

Sometimes it isn't the actual sadness itself but the fear of the sadness that makes Julie feel as if she's sinking. She's aware that there is no water here on West Seventy-Seventh Street, but still, this is how it feels to her, the darkness waves in and over her. All-consuming.

At times, when it's really bad, when she can't figure out what there is left to hope for or even what can actually come from any of that hope, life, the mere idea of living, of caring, of walking with her son to the market seems impossible.

So thank God for her Zoloft, for that modest blue pill. With a bit of luck it will save her, at least fix the little something that's a bit off in her brain. Maybe one day she will be able to breathe easily again. Because she hasn't always been like this, has she?

It doesn't matter how long it's been or hasn't been. The important thing is that she will be able to invest in the world, in her life, in her child, without shutting down. She will be able to experience emotions again. This is the promise. If she continues to take her medicine and go to therapy she will be able to feel without falling apart.

After that there should be no need for the numbness that crowded her head that day, making her beg for death. Or the persistent drone that continues to shadow her, even right now, even as she successfully strolls down the street with her son.

Okay, chicken breast. Julie has changed her mind and decided to go to Westside Market, where they have everything in the same store. This should be easier. She searches, chicken breast, aisle two. Look how many different kinds. She should find natural breasts, hormone-free, no antibiotics, but she will buy these Perdue ones. She reads the package. Four skinless breasts. More than enough. Now, breadcrumbs. Breadcrumbs are up above the chicken. Flavored or unflavored? Flavored. Great. Eggs. And so on.

There is this problem of where to put the food. Julie looks around the market. She finds another mother with a stroller who interestingly enough is piling the food around her baby. Julie places the chicken and the container of breadcrumbs on top of Teddy's blanket. She puts the eggs to the right of his legs. This must be okay to do. Julie looks at the other mother again to reassure herself. Fine, this is absolutely fine.

And this is exciting. Ethan is going to be so happy. A home-cooked meal. Julie is staring at the bottled water now and trying to decide which to buy. There are all different sizes. She looks into the stroller. Only one bottle can fit. She locates the quart size, .99 cents for one. $1.99 for another. All of a sudden her head feels funny. She tells herself to calm down. This is only a bottle of water we're talking about here. She will pull a bottle off the shelf. Any bottle. She will choose it this way. She closes her eyes, reaches her arm out for a bottle.

But she can't.

Her eyes open, and she is here. In this brightly lit supermarket. It is too dark outside now. Too late to cook dinner. Too many people rushing up and down these aisles. She's scared she might faint, and if she faints, someone might take Teddy and if someone takes Teddy...

Breathe.

People are looking at her now. They can see, can't they, see that she is falling apart? She pushes forward. She will empty the stroller and pay for what she has. She will tell Ethan to bring home bottled water or just use water from the tap.

She looks down at the stroller and it's all wrong. It is too low to the ground. There are dogs outside and it's too dirty. She lifts Teddy into her arms. She is moving.

"Hey, lady!" she hears behind her.

She keeps moving. She is watching her feet so that she doesn't trip. She is spinning. This is what she'll say. *Someone took the carriage.* That's it. She had Teddy in a grocery cart. And someone took the carriage. And by the time she realized whoever it was was gone. So of course she had to put the food back. And she is running. And.

And there is another one of these inside her now. Another one of these lives. She keeps moving. *Up this same damn hill. Is there—is a man hiding behind the stoop of that brownstone? No*, she thinks, stopping herself. *This is a trick your mind is playing on you.*

It's okay, she is walking now. Slow. But *ha ha, you are pregnant.* Each time she starts to calm she hears that voice. That same skeptical, mocking, bitter person furious she is alive.

She is hurrying again, passing the basketball courts and Isabella's and the shoe store and now she, one two three four more awnings and she's home.

Chinese takeout is always the easiest to order because there is something for everyone. Ethan likes peanut butter noodles and chicken with broccoli. Georgie is of course an "I'll take anything," and Julie can get her meal steamed. No oil, no salt.

The food is delivered hot and they sit facing each other. Georgie has set the table. There are forks and knives. Tall glasses filled with icy cold Perrier. Teddy is in his high chair bathed and ready to go to sleep. Ethan unwraps a Yodel and puts two candles in it. There is always next year, Julie tells herself as she watches Ethan light it.

These are the innumerable ways she fails. And will continue to fail. Even on the medicine she hadn't been able to cook dinner or bake her son a chocolate cake.

"Happy birthday to you." Julie is singing out loud with Ethan and Georgie. Teddy clapping his hands. "Happy birthday to you."

This is the family now. "Happy birthday, dear Teddy. Happy birthday…" Julie hears her voice and only her voice as she watches Ethan and Georgie help her son blow out the two candles burning before him.

She is praying out loud for his future. Yet all she can think to say is, "Make a wish, my love."

FIFTEEN

"What is *real*?" asked the Rabbit one day, when they were lying side by side near the nursery fender, before Nana came to tidy the room. "Does it mean having things that buzz inside you and a stick-out handle?" This is the part Julie is looking for:

"Real isn't how you are made," said the Skin Horse. "It's a thing that happens to you. When a child loves you for a long, long time, not just to play with, but *really* loves you, then you become Real."

"Does it hurt?" asked the Rabbit.

"Sometimes," said the Skin Horse, for he was always truthful. "When you are Real you don't mind being hurt."

The television is on and Ethan is in the bathroom. Julie doesn't have much time. He will join her in bed soon. Try to catch *Howard* or the news. Maybe read a few pages from a book or the end of a magazine article he hadn't the chance to finish in the bath. Julie touches her old book and remembers herself as she was when she first heard it.

She consciously misses this part of herself. The little girl with the knobby knees. The little girl she would have wanted to grow into if things had been different.

It is only a matter of minutes, tens of minutes at the most, until the television is clicked off. Then the lights. At best, Ethan will say "I love you" as he rolls over for sleep. And then silence.

There are a few last splashes here and there. Julie hears him rise out of the tub. He must be standing, toweling himself dry. She imagines he is rubbing the terrycloth between his legs, now comes the talcum powder. The bathroom door opens and he is in the room. Another pair of white pajamas. Another night.

"What are you reading?" he asks, looking at the book Julie is holding between her hands.

"Just an old book of mine my mother found for Teddy."

"That's nice."

Ethan is at the foot of their bed, walking toward his side. He looks at the television and clicks it off. Tonight it is a magazine.

Julie closes the book and stares at the ceiling. She will just say it. She will say the words, "I am pregnant," and wait for his reaction. She will say the words, "I am pregnant," and abide him. Let him make the decision of whether or not they keep this baby.

Now is as good a time as any. She waits for him to finish with his magazine. He turns and looks at her, at the still soft lines that make up her face.

"Honey?" he asks.

"Yeah." Julie inches toward him.

"I just wanted you to know that dinner was nice."

Her eyes move from the buttons of his pajama top to the embroidered edging of the sheets.

"No, it wasn't. I—"

"No, it was," he says, angling himself into a position that forces her to look at him.

"I wanted to make the dinner. I wanted to bake Teddy a cake."

"You had bad luck at the market. Don't be so hard on yourself." His hand is on her shoulder now. Somehow he is still able to believe in good and bad luck. In sports teams, in story books, in an extra fucking birthday candle.

Julie has told him she is pregnant and he is kissing her. A small brave kiss on her cheek.

His lips are cautious, giving her the space to move away if she might need to. Julie lifts her head up and takes a breath. His lips press against her neck, and then again. Now they are running along her shoulder bone. One kiss, then another. He stops every so often to check her reaction. Her eyes are shut. Her body light. She arches to greet him, to make it easier for him. She wants to be taken. "Take me," she whispers.

They are scared. Julie is never not aware that this is about fear. This love that they are making bound in all that was lost between them. Both of them knowing that it can never be how it was. Their legs entwined, he moves within her. She feels him. This is good. This is better than not feeling.

She is holding him. Her wrists heavy around his neck. Her body loyal. She is moving with him. Back and forth. Fiercely, desperately. She is begging for forgiveness. A forgiveness she knows she can never accept.

Ethan is reading to her. She is in his arms, starting over.

"*The Velveteen Rabbit*, by Margery Williams. There was once a Velveteen Rabbit, and in the beginning he was really splendid."

Ethan's voice is warm, peaceful. Her body calms. She is happy that she told him. The tears are gone and she is breathing. In, she holds it and it stays. Out, she lets go and it disappears. She is making progress.

"Does it happen all at once, like being wound up," he asked, "or bit by bit?"

"It doesn't happen all at once," said the Skin Horse. "You become. It takes a long time. That's why it doesn't often happen to people who break easily, or have sharp edges, or who have to be carefully kept. Generally, by the time you are Real, most of your hair has been loved off, and your eyes drop out and you get loose in the joints and very shabby. But these things don't matter at all, because once you are Real you can't be ugly, except to people who don't understand."

Julie is resting on her side. She looks so peaceful at this very moment that if you were only to glance at her you'd know. Know she was a little girl trained to fall asleep in the arms of her hero.

She opens her eyes. Ethan is still lying next to her, his head cupped in his hand, the weight of his whole body resting on his elbow. He is staring at her. The intensity of his belief is embarrassing.

"Baby," he says, "you're going to make it through this. We're going to make it through this."

He touches her cheek as he says this. His gentle fingers pushing back the bits of hair that are hiding her face. Here he is, still just a boy. He is talking, they will keep the baby, everything will work out, how nice for Teddy. He is promising her he can deliver redemption. If Julie can play her part she will emerge a girl able to balance air under her feet, a woman.

"You really think so?" Julie asks as they cling to each other. She wants to believe that Ethan holds this truth that has invariably shunned her.

So she lives out his fairy-tale. With tears in her eyes.

SIXTEEN

There are two doctors. Dr. Salzman, the gynecologist, who says it's okay, the medicine. That he's had many patients who took antidepressants throughout their pregnancies, their babies are normal. Normal birth weight, normal development.

"I have at least eight expectant women on antidepressants as we speak."

Dr. Salzman talks to Ethan man to man: "One out of every seven women experience some degree of depression after they give birth." These kind of statistics are mixed in with, "How 'bout those Knicks?"

But then there's Dr. Edelman, who says she's not sure. That there haven't been long enough studies on these newer antidepressants. That they are still not even sure what Zoloft does to the brain tissue of the person taking the medication, let alone a fetus.

"It is possible that antidepressants can mess with the fetus's synapses and the baby can—"

"What does this mean?" Ethan interrupts. Julie is embarrassed by the hostility in his voice.

"It means that we are still in the early stages of understanding the full effect of these psychotropic medicines. There have been a few studies. Offspring of mothers who took these older antidepressants while pregnant. These studies suggest that there hasn't been any negative outcome. But we just don't know."

Julie is proud of her doctor. Dr. Edelman is able to keep her composure. Ethan's antagonism doesn't shake her in the least. She is a wife, a mother, a doctor.

"So it's really up to the two of you to weigh the risk. Julie's depression is chronic. And I'd certainly suggest—strongly suggest—that she starts back up on the medication as soon as she gives birth. The upside is that the hormones the body makes while pregnant often mitigate depression. I think that for the term of her pregnancy she should be okay."

Ethan still doesn't understand. He continues berating her with questions. He wants to know why the gynecologist thinks it's okay, while she's unsure. He is mad. Mad at the pharmaceutical companies for not knowing, at Dr. Edelman for prescribing medication in the first place. He doesn't understand how this could happen when Julie wore her diaphragm.

Julie watches Ethan's body fold into itself. She's never seen him like this. Ethan is a person who measures every word, every action. Even when she was in the hospital he was polite, never hysterical. But here, in Dr. Edelman's office, he is like any other person, anxious to find fault, attribute blame.

Of course it's not Dr. Edelman's doing that she and Ethan find themselves here. It's not even Ethan's, other than in the technical sense. But none of that matters. They are in this office, faced with a series of decisions. Julie takes or doesn't take the Zoloft while she's pregnant. They keep or don't keep this baby. Julie hears the words swirl around in her head. She can't believe it: keep or don't keep. How did their love become a choice?

It was one of the last warm days. Just before the leaves begin to turn for fall. She was wearing light denim jean shorts, cut just above the center of her thigh. A black T-shirt. She held the jar of bubbles between her hands and blew. Small, see-through balls disbanded slowly into the air. It was the magic hour. Just before dinner, the sky, a sapphire blue. She is on her back, her head resting in Ethan's lap; one of his hands was touching her shoulder, the other waving a plastic wand above her face.

Any passerby—a student, a professor, the guy selling sandwiches out of a cooler—anyone who happened to catch a look at the pair, lounging on the campus green, laughing, blowing bubbles would have bet their life on it. That these two would win.

Ethan holds Julie's hand. They are on the street, walking to a coffee shop. The victory peaches, only two days old, seem a distant memory. They are as far away as those jean shorts. Ethan's coat is pressed, his shoes clean, newly soled. He opens the door for her, takes a table, pulls out a chair. He is what he appears to be, everything he ever promised.

Their meals come. A nice big burger and fries for him. Some toast, dry, a few packets of jelly for her. Julie watches Ethan take a large bite and chew. He has always been a fast eater and she has come to depend on this. On their meals being over quickly.

"It's a little rare," he says, turning the burger toward her. "Do I have to send it back?"

Julie inspects his mark. "I don't think so."

He stops and takes a sip of Coke. "Remember that girl who David dated? The one who went on and on about the 'format' of a veggie burger?"

Julie smiles as she sticks her teeth into the bread. Ethan is kind, trying to lighten the conversation. But she's okay with her meal. Toasted rye bread can't hurt her. She is no different than their son. One new food a week.

"Thank God they broke up," Julie says. "Remember how disgusted she was by the size of me?"

Julie gained over twenty-five pounds with Teddy. She struggled with eating throughout the pregnancy, but she gained the necessary weight. An egg for breakfast. A turkey sandwich for lunch.

"You were your most beautiful," Ethan says, still chewing. Julie passes him a napkin. I will do even better this time, she tells herself. She watches him take his last bite. I will even try ice cream again, not fat free but real ice cream, if he lets me keep this baby.

"Well, it's eight months we are talking about here." He is dabbing the napkin to his mouth, looking at her, his eyes with her eyes. She accepts his sizing her up. In fact, she feels relieved. Let him determine whether or not she is a fit enough specimen for the task at hand.

"Do you think you can do it?" he asks.

This is the tricky part. If she says, "Yes," then Ethan will think she is strong. Maybe he'll stay with her. Maybe a new baby will make it worth it to him to carry on. But if she says, "No." If she says, "No, I'm too scared of myself," he will sooner or later, not today, not tomorrow, not for another ten years perhaps, but if she says, "No, I can't have your baby," he will ultimately leave her.

What keeps a man? If you're lucky, the children. Her mother said this countless times. To a certain kind of man the family is sacrosanct. But what happens if this man takes a lover and the lover can produce? Even worse, what if his lover wears a bikini and swims with him? Her father isn't the only man who likes to swim.

Ethan's lover swims to him. Her arms toned from the weights she lifts before work, the yoga on Thursdays, the Latin dancing she takes Sunday afternoons. She swims, her fingers painted to match her toes. She is careful to be elegant, no red polish, careful not to be a cliché.

She swims this way, head above the flow, hair dry. Southern California is a far cry from where she comes from. Back home five bucks gets you a beer and as much Banana Boat as you want. Here it's twelve, thirteen bucks for a Bloody Mary, thirty-two for a tube of Bain de Soleil, forget the cost of a cabana.

Julie waits in bed. Ethan is back at work, thirty floors above ground, making decisions, affecting other people's lives. Fortunately, Teddy and Georgie are at a playdate. Julie is alone. Her room dark. Her head keeps silent this way.

She turns from the wall and faces the bathroom. Imagine if she could do this? If Dr. Edelman really thinks she can handle going off the medication, can you imagine? She could give back to Ethan, give him another child, give Teddy a little brother or sister. She takes a deep breath, gives herself a second chance.

Ethan leaps into the pool and wets the girlfriend. His splash louder than the memory of his children's laughter, but not to worry. He'll be back home before they know it. He had to go to L.A. for business. What's an extra day or two? No harm no foul.

The girlfriend bobs up and down. She teases him: submerging herself for a second or two. She stays under just long enough to make him caution. Then she reappears, arms open, teeth whiter than her bikini top.

There is an implicit threat to it all. Julie looks down at her stomach. There is an implicit threat to this bit of beauty, of hope, of whatever it is floating inside her decay.

SEVENTEEN

Julie takes a seat in the rocking chair, Teddy in her arms. She looks up at his changing table and swallows. This pregnancy the nausea is worse. But it's easy retribution considering.

Although the weepiness does get to her at times. The streams of mostly uncalled-for tears that seem to flow from her eyes are, for lack of a better word, embarrassing. Never mind though, in a few short months Julie will start taking her medicine again. In a few short months all of these various discomforts will seem like a dream.

But poor Ethan, he's having a hard time. He gapes at her from across the dinner table, from the other side of the bed. He's not entirely comfortable with their decision to keep the baby. In the end, though, it's her body.

So Julie spends a lot of time reassuring him: Yes, he's absolutely right, they are tears that he sees dripping down her face, but they're not sad tears. This rationale doesn't seem to do much good, but she persists. "Don't tell me," she's said, attempting to make fun, "that you've never heard of hopeful tears?"

Is she hopeful? Mostly she is. It's hard for Julie to imagine that she nearly missed, she sniffs Teddy's pants, how stinky, a life with him. And the baby in her belly, she stands and carries Teddy over to his changing table, the baby in her belly is probably a lucky thing too.

Julie swears there's a logic to all that has happened. This pregnancy is surely a sign from God. If not God who else? But even for the sake of argument, say it's not God. This life growing inside of her is certainly an endorsement of a certain kind, a backing for continuance, something like that.

Teddy is kicking his legs, fighting with her. He's angry and annoyed but she'll change her son's diaper even if he doesn't like her for it. She pulls down his pants, his diaper heavy, she opens it, full as can be.

Julie is almost envious of Teddy's bowel movement. Both he and Ethan go to the bathroom daily, while she hasn't taken a shit in two or three days. Constipation isn't unusual with pregnancy. She knows this but still she wants desperately to go to the bathroom. She feels too full, her stomach way too distended for only fourteen weeks.

Teddy settles, gives into being wiped down. Julie smiles. It must be natural, the impulse to feel clean. A wave of nausea overcomes her; she takes a breath and swallows. Teddy begins kicking at her again. She lifts him off the table and plants him on his feet. He's a sturdy little guy. Julie prays he is able to stay this way forever: strong legs to support his frame, powerful legs to help carry him through.

She should hurry. Ethan will be downstairs in a minute to pick them up. They have a car now, a Ford Explorer they're keeping parked on Amsterdam. It's nice having a car. They take Teddy for day trips, drive out to the mall. In fact, Ethan likes being away from the city so much that he wants them to move.

He has a list of reasons why living in the suburbs will be a better life for them: Teddy will have a backyard with a jungle gym, will be able to ride his bike on the street. They'll have more room too, for all his stuff, her stuff, toys. Not to mention safety.

Ethan is being nice about the whole thing: of course they could stay in the city if she wants to. He will, in the end, do whatever makes her happy. But nevertheless there's a lot of selling going on.

"What do you have here?" is a frequently asked question. Julie finds it hard to answer him. It's not like she has a job, or is one of those women who takes advantage of the culture the city has to offer, the big group of friends, the Wednesday matinee, the lunches. Every once in a while she and Ethan go to the movies, grab a quick bite, but that's it really. Her various doctors are here, but as Ethan says, she can drive into the city if she has to.

Julie laughs and grabs the diaper bag. She nudges Teddy to move out the door and locks the apartment. With one hand she takes his in hers and holds it. With her other she presses for the elevator. She nearly laughs again. Ethan must be crazy, drive into the city.

But why not? It couldn't be harder than any of the other things she's been asking of herself. At any rate, today is just another exploratory trip, and who cares where they are as long as she has her Sundays back.

Julie buzzes for the elevator again, she still can't believe it, today every feeding, every diaper change is hers. Georgie has started taking Sundays off and it's wonderful. On Sundays, with Ethan driving them along, they are the family Julie wants them to be.

"Anyway you're from Jersey, you grew up with all this, you get it." Ethan turns off at the exit. Julie is in the front seat, looking out the passenger window. Teddy is sleeping in the back. She's listening to her husband talk, but really she's daydreaming about the movies she's been watching lately, mostly old black-and-white films. In the city all she has to do is call the video store and within an hour a tape is delivered to her door.

She steals something from each film: a smile, a laugh, a wink of the eye. It's a safe little world Julie's gradually creating. In this world all men come home. Just like Fredric March, they drop their bag and open their arms. It's an odd thing actually. If you bother watching them you find out that most of what people say about the old movies is true. Rita Hayworth really was beautiful.

Ethan double-parks along the side of the road. Julie watches him as he runs into the office to get their real-estate agent. Nice guy, Ethan. Julie unbuckles herself and twists around to Teddy, still sleeping in his car seat. She turns back around and waits. She can make a world for herself here too, can't she? She looks outside, cute town. There must be lots of things to do here. It doesn't have to be tennis.

The real estate agent brakes, pulls ahead, brakes again. A huge map spread across her dash. Ethan is cursing her as he follows her car. "How stupid can she be?" It's their third time going out with this broker and she drives him crazy, always stopping to check directions, or getting lost, or rolling down her window to say something neither of them need to know: "Follow me, it gets a little tricky here, so pay attention."

Her skin is unnaturally dark for the season, her cheeks sunken. "She's an idiot," Ethan says when she brakes again.

"At least she's trying," Julie answers in the woman's defense. "My mom would have been great at this."

"That's true," Ethan brakes again. "Much better than this broad."

Julie is holding a picture of the house they are on their way to see. Already, they have accumulated enough of these pretty brochures to kindle a small fire. This one says:

5 Hillbrook Road. A secluded country lane leads to this wonderful brick manor situated on two of Brookville's finest acres. Lawns and specimen plantings. A thirty-minute commute to the city. Jericho School System ranked top in New York State. A perfect family home.

"You play golf, don't you?" the broker asks Ethan as she opens the front door.

"Sure."

"Well, my husband is the president of Cedar Oaks. Which is just down the road from here. I'm sure he'd be more than happy to show you around the place. You know, it's a very hard club to get into but he can help."

"So let's see." She flicks on the lights. "Spacious foyer, I must say, gracious details throughout." She directs her attention to Julie. "Wait until you see this kitchen. What potential."

Ethan, Julie, Teddy, and the real estate broker are all in the kitchen of 5 Hillbrook Road. "You know," the broker says, tapping the glass, "these old St. Charles cabinets have become quite a collector's item."

This house is nice. It has gray shutters. A large backyard where Julie and Ethan can put a pool. On the kitchen table there are pictures of the house in spring. White tulips line the walkway. There is a cherry blossom tree to the right of the front door.

Julie will be a housewife here. I am a housewife in the city, she reminds herself as she runs her hand across the red vinyl countertop. The kitchen will have to be redone and each of the bathrooms. Three baths and the kitchen, but other than that all this house seems to need is a paint job.

"What a sunny kitchen," the broker keeps going. "What a great place to raise some orchids."

Ethan takes Julie by the hand. "May we walk around the yard?" he asks the broker.

"Of course." She opens the kitchen door and Teddy, who is now wide awake, bolts.

"Orchids?" Ethan whispers into Julie's ear. They smile at each other and step outside. Look at their son scampering across this frozen lawn. His run is awkward but he's running nevertheless. In front of the kitchen window is an even patch of land, perfect for one of those large jungle gym sets.

"You know," Ethan says as they watch him. He pulls her closer to him, rests his hand on her belly, "We can make a happy life here."

There is quiet and then the sound of a train rumbling in the near distance. "I know," Julie says, still looking at their boy, "we could."

"I'm going to marry you one day," Ethan promised the first night they made love, "and we're going to have babies and a house and we're going to be happy. Making you happy will be my job in life. When people ask me what I do I will tell them, 'I make Julie happy.'"

"Really?"

"Really," he said, leaning over to kiss her.

"Well, you won't have to do much. Just being with you makes me happy." Julie remembers burying her head within the tangled hair of his underarm, man's hair. The smell of him late at night growing familiar. The smell of her father diminishing.

"You know, I want to be happy."

"Of course you do, baby," he said, holding her. "Everyone wants to be happy."

They are passing the garage now. Ethan is talking plans. He bends down and lifts Teddy up onto his shoulders, grasps his little feet to steady him. Ethan's free arm is hanging over Julie's shoulder. As he directs her round the side of the house he explains, "This house is the right place at the right price and with interest rates so low we'll be able to lock in a good mortgage."

He keeps going, "We'll have it painted, put in a new kitchen for you, and look, we can put a hoop here for me and the little guy."

Ethan is pointing to an area just to the right of the garage. He is smiling. He is beaming. He is beautiful, her husband.

At this moment, as Julie hugs her leather coat against her expanded self, she believes that it is all forgotten.

"What color should we paint our shutters?" she asks.

EIGHTEEN

The girls in the audience all look the same. It's hard for Julie to believe that most of these girls are actually younger than she is. They seem older. No, "older" isn't exactly the right word. It's more that they seem to know what they want in a way Julie has never even bothered to ask herself.

Who knew to go to Yale, or to spend a semester abroad on a fishing boat? Marriage and babies, marriage and babies were all Julie ever really considered. This is not to say that she didn't know about Gloria Steinem. She knew all about the ERA, but somehow it didn't apply to her.

Although there was a moment in time when Julie thought she might want to go to Berkeley. She was big into social justice and Berkeley seemed like the right place. But it was a reach. Still, she buckled down, worked hard in school, studied diligently for her SATs. The only problem was that in doing so she had gained a little weight.

"Pretty girls like you grow up, get married, have babies."

"What does that have to do with it, Mom?"

She remembers her mother looking at her as if this was simply beyond her comprehension, what does it have to do with it? "It has to do with the fact that no matter what he might say no great guy wants a girl with an extra ten pounds on her." She paused, "No matter how smart she is."

Julie didn't take it personally, her mother wasn't being malicious, she was simply importing the truth as she saw it.

It was only after Julie married that she began to grasp how wrong her mother was. Even in light of the whole "biological clock" Julie had a good fifteen years she could have put into becoming someone. Certainly more than enough time to lose those ten pounds.

Ethan takes a sip of his Jack and Coke. "How was the little guy today?"

This is the way it is now: nice, easy. The uncomfortable moments between them are fewer and farther between. He is trying his best, coming home from work by eight almost every night. She is trying her best too. They just had dinner at a quaint Italian place in the West Village. Now they're at the Bitter End, waiting to see her brother perform.

Julie rubs her belly. It isn't that she regrets being Teddy's mother or Ethan's wife. She's excited about their future, eager to move to their new home, anxious to have this baby. But she can't help herself from wondering.

She looks from one face to the next. What is it exactly? It's not the glitter eye shadow or platform shoes. Not the professional girls with their briefcases. She can't pinpoint the matter except to say it has to do with hair color as much as anything else. What is life like for that girl over there with the flamingo-pink hair? What would life be like if she were to become Julie Davis, the girl with flamingo-pink hair?

She can see it. The movers will pull into her newly purchased house thirty miles out of the city. She'll be standing there to greet them.

"What's a girl like you doing in a place like this?" one of the moving men ask her.

"Boys," she'll say, passing out beers, her pink hair flying free, "I'm a covert warrior in suburbia."

They'll laugh.

She'll put too much sugar in the cupcakes she makes for the bake sales, wear sweats, Birkenstocks with socks. She'll even let her arm hair grow.

It will be fun when that damn Allison or Debbie, some damn woman with a name like that saunters over to her sports utility vehicle. Debbie all smooth with her: *how's Teddy enjoying school* and *is there anything I can do for you...* her ostensible kiss peppered with all the authenticity of a well-trained house frau.

And Julie won't disappoint. She'll play her part with aplomb, whipping out a high-powered electric vibrator from her glove compartment and swinging it. Brave ol' Debbie won't know what to do, scampering away from the car in her salmon-colored JP Tods.

"I'm a covert warrior in suburbia, Deb." Julie will laugh a laugh more wicked than Ani DiFranco. What are you scared of, Debbie? Ridiculous woman, running away, her Kelly bag smacking at her hip.

Julie is suspicious of women with mauve-painted toenails. She doesn't trust them scampering around in their pleated pants, diamond studs flashing. So busy they are with their kids, their homes, their Pilates. Although she herself spends most of her time preoccupied by the same issues: what color to make the baby's room, where to put her new gas range, does she need a guest room.

There is another world. A world where women travel to St. Barts for the weekend, live with men but pay for their own sushi. Fine, Julie has achieved what she set out to, she married a nice young man. But now what?

There was one night, just after she and Ethan married, a Christmas party at Au Bar. Some colleague of Ethan's, a woman lawyer, midthirties, came by their table. Julie stood, did the wifely nice to meet you, heard so much about you thing. And the woman responded appropriately, reached out her arm. Nice to meet you too.

But as they shook hands the gulf between them was clear. Julie could squeeze and squeeze and still never come close to matching the firmness of the woman's grip. How could she, with the other holding complete advantage?

It remains a puzzle to Julie. How did that woman rise above? No, that's not really the question, is it. It's more how did she, Julie, allow herself to fall short. After all, she was aware, as aware as anyone, that being taken care of came at a price.

David lights a smoke and begins to play. In the beginning it was just what it was. A little boy newly released from red bifocals, tinkering with a guitar. It was Julie's guitar first, but she never inhabited it, never cradled it to her chest, never begged of it in the way he begs of it.

Here he goes, playing for twenty people. He stops to check, same number of strings, same noise. He leans over his instrument, a bit of hair falling over his eyes. His melodies echo with familiarity, the sound of their father's car easing into the driveway. The sound of Eddie Van Halen laughing. So this is how Julie finds her brother. All these years later, still practicing.

David's hands are much more beautiful than her own, as is his face—sculpted, shadowed. He moves his long fingers, stretching them against the neck of this hope he is bound to. Gently, forcefully he manipulates his world. This, the only world in which he feels safe.

Julie winces. Her brother is waging a war up on that dimly lit stage. Each chord battling to defeat the actual sound of his heartache.

At home Ethan is hyper. He wants more from her. Julie brushes her teeth and feels him studying her body. She doesn't want this. Not tonight. Tonight she feels heavy with baby. Hasn't she done enough already?

She continues brushing her teeth, reapplies deodorant under her arms. She is ready for whatever tonight's sex will entail. Although she hopes it's fast. In, out, over.

This is precisely what happens. He's in her, getting off. It's not anything other than a dick in a cunt. Servicing is the kind of sex she's grown accustomed to. It isn't that she doesn't love him. She does love Ethan. She'll do what she has to do in order to make him come.

It's just that she doesn't love him painfully. At least not in the way that lets you take it in the ass until you're bleeding. The way that makes you want to cut your wrists, bake cookies. Sometimes, late at night, Julie lays awake in bed and touches herself. Part of her longs for that kind of want. The wanting that reinforces that you're not good enough. That you'll never be good enough. The wanting that lets you know your dreams are impossible even as you're living them.

Julie is in the bathroom, wiping the come off her vagina. She examines her growing belly, mounting thighs. In a few weeks she won't be able to see over her stomach. She'll have to rely on the mirror. But tonight she bears witness to everything. Julie lifts the flesh of her breast up toward her face. Her nipples are the size of silver dollar pancakes. She had forgotten about this. How much they spread. How dark and bumpy they get when pregnant.

She turns to look at the two thick blue lines that have begun protruding from her left leg. She follows the bulging veins from the backside of her knee down her calf until they stop just an inch or two above her ankle. They are a new thing. Something Julie's sure belong only on old people. Nevertheless, when she looks at her feet she smiles. She gets a kick out of them. Just having nice toes makes her luckier than most people.

Julie is doing this amusing little thing. She has tweezers and she's digging with them. She is on the toilet now. Her panties are down, and she's very busy, tunneling through her pubic hair, probing for ingrowns. She finds a hair and pulls at it. It stings, but the sting is okay. She takes another stab.

She is getting the hairs out. Slowly but surely she is cleaning up this area. Soon there will be no more blood, no more mess. Julie is worrying about socks. She rearranged Ethan's socks earlier in the day and realizes now, from atop the toilet bowl, that he needs a pair of gray socks. He doesn't have gray socks. And Teddy needs new sneakers. New sneakers for Teddy, gray socks for Ethan.

She is burrowing the tweezers under her skin. She sees herself shaking hands with her decorator, instructing him to have their new home painted white, every room white. She has decided to become a minimalist.

Okay, tomorrow. She is making a mental note as she pokes around. Pick up sneakers, socks. Decide on paint color: Linen White, Atrium White, Super White.

Next, Julie pictures herself smiling wide for Ethan's family. She'll look nice in the silk ensemble she bought on sale at Barneys. A size twelve but it works, the pants are elastic, the blouse loose. She better make sure her shoes still fit with her ankles this swollen. Shoes, though, are easy, around the corner, a hundred bucks.

Julie feels powerful. Her hormones are working. She's plugging along through this pregnancy. *I am the last doll to the left in the window of FAO Schwarz. I am the ballerina.*

She continues digging. More blood comes. She pretends she's not worried about this yet.

NINETEEN

"Mommy," Teddy giggles at the sight of her coloring. She is coloring him a house. A house with plum shutters and an orange front door. He is picking the colors. One by one he lifts them off the table: melon, orchid, robin's egg blue. He watches her in amazement. She is creating a world for him in which to live. Julie is conscious of this as she draws, conscious that she is the one responsible for producing a likeness of his happiness.

Julie is enjoying coloring. There's not much else to do today. So she's taking her time. She's adding flowers to the granny smith apple front lawn, scattered spots of carnation pink. Rain knocks against the windowpane. It is another slow winter afternoon. But tomorrow will be a busy day. Julie looks around the apartment. They are all packed up, just some odds and ends, the few essentials they need for the night. Teddy is pulling at her arm, insisting that she stay focused. He demands this of her, demands that she remain in the present.

Julie turns toward her son and kisses the top of his head. She is grateful for this demand. The difficulty of staying in the present with Teddy, of not disappearing inside herself, reveals how often she does turn inward. She has allowed years to dissolve this way. That same blank numbness passing for time.

Teddy hands her a crayon and points. "Sure, honey," Julie says filling in the sun. To Teddy's eye the sun is dandelion yellow.

Julie listens to the easy pattering of the rain against her window, the cars outside sloshing through the puddles. She's not entirely sure why she and Ethan are moving, what they hope to gain twenty-five miles east of here. She feels her growing baby shift.

Fifteen, twenty more hours and this part of Julie's life, this time here on West Seventy-Seventh Street will dissolve into memory. New York untouched, a new store, a co-op being resurfaced, another moving truck. Julie leaves no vacancy, no one to miss her. Hardly anyone will even notice she's gone.

Perhaps this is as good a reason as any to try the suburbs. Maybe on the North Shore of Long Island Julie will make friends. Just one friend, one good girl friend to pal around with, another mother, how nice. They could take the kids to the park, to playgroup. They could go to Saks, share a frozen yogurt, busy their little boys with French fries and talk. Gossip, how much fun would gossip be?

Her mother always had a slew of these friends. There was her redheaded friend Bobbie, their neighbor Mrs. Rennert. Julie's mother was eternally popular, always beautiful, always a great personality.

Harriet found a way to befriend all sorts of people. So that with the plumber it became "be there in five," the pipe unclogged, a cup of coffee, a question or two about how his wife Jane was. The electrician, "give me twenty," and within a half an hour the kitchen lights were working again, a cookie and out the door. She even managed to get the drycleaner to drop off and pick up from their home, which at the time was more than unusual. And to top it all off there was a butcher.

Julie stops coloring, what was his name, was it Harry, Ben? She can picture his slightly stained apron. He always gave her a lollipop, always double-bagged and then twisted the meat closed. Julie sees her mother as she is now, pacing up and down the aisle of D'Agostino; a half a crab cake works fine, a small bottle of Perrier. No need for Harry, for the finest cut of beef tenderloin, for hardly anything these aisles offer.

She palms a crayon Teddy has handed her. The same maca-roni and cheese orange he picked earlier for the front door. She checks her watch. Her mother is probably just getting back from having her hair blown out. What a night for a date. Julie returns her attention to the paper before her. She doesn't want to think about her mother dating. What it means. What acts her mother will be asked to perform.

First there was the asshole from East Hampton who liked to watch her mop. She would cook him dinner, put the dishes in the dishwasher and begin mopping for him. Back and forth. This turned him on until it didn't. She got sick over him, sores around her calves, fevers.

Next Harriet dated a stockbroker who played the piano on Sundays. He collected cream cheese and other white things on the sides of his mouth. She liked his eyes. Thought she was dating Paul McCartney, pushed the fact that he was a cold caller out of her mind. When he left her for a wealthier divorcee she increased her dosage of anti-anxiety medication and got a stron-ger sleeping pill.

Most recently she dated some accountant who'd had an affair with his dying wife's nurse. Her mother found him erudite because that's how he described himself. She started talking about wine and things that go along with such conversation. Wine, violence in modern cinema, Blacks.

The high point of their whole thing was a trip to a discount department store in Westchester where he bought her an Armani suit. She said good-bye to him when he asked her to contribute fifty-fifty to the relationship. "Did he really expect me to go Dutch at this point in my life?"

Anyway, this new guy is supposed to be nice, a garmento widower. A widower is what her mother is looking for now. "A widower," Harriet's explained to her daughter, "is a man who actually likes being married."

"What do you think, honey?" Julie is holding the paper up for Teddy to judge. His eyes focus in. After a pause there is a big smile. He begins clapping. Julie grabs him, "I love you so much, baby."

She gets up off the ground and walks him over to Georgie. "Look at what Teddy drew, Georgie." Julie has come to accept and to some extent even appreciate leaving him with her. This is when the nausea comes, now, in the late afternoon. She can't believe it's still every day, and to think she's almost six months into her pregnancy.

In bed Julie faces the wall. She can handle nausea much more easily than actually throwing up. Throwing up reminds her of who she was. It's hard for her to imagine that she ever forced herself to throw up. But she did. That and many other things.

She glances at the porcelain figurine on her bedside table. Her father had given it to her as a little girl. A princess stepping into her horsedrawn chariot. It doesn't matter. Julie rolls deeper into herself. She must push past her disillusion. Funny word but that's what it is, utter and total disillusion.

Her father based his departure on pizza. Twenty-seven years of marriage and he explained it this way, "Your mother likes the fancy kind of pizza with the thin crust, and I am just a regular pizza guy, thick crust, lots of cheese."

Obviously, there was more to the story than his affinity for cheese, but he ran with this cheese/crust thing for several months, during which time he frequented sports bars in central Jersey with whoever that one was. With her, he was a man of the people, a Democrat, a Michelob drinker.

You are not to blame. Yes I am. No you're not.

If Julie stayed at home, they probably would have continued, at least for a little while longer, as a family. Each in their own way pretending to be happy. But to what extent her marrying Ethan is to blame for her parents' separation is anyone's guess. Her mother would say her father wanted a shiksa. The only difference between him and most men his age being that he went out and got one. Ron would argue that he just couldn't stand it any more. That they have different values, the whole thick versus thin crust thing.

Julie has come to accept that there is no one truth. Her father always wanted a young girl and in one way or another always kept one. Her mother had been wearing fur for years. One more mink wasn't significant, certainly not enough to mark a breaking point. The more Julie goes over this, the more convinced she becomes. Disillusion is inevitability. And those moments of magic are just that, magic.

She must never imbue the white picket fence as an affirmation of the good in the world. In all fairness, her mother didn't know any better. She was vigilant to her faith. She had that fence sanded down and repainted every spring.

But Julie does know better. She must take the good as it comes, appreciate it for what it is and not ask for more. If God gives her a second healthy baby, if he lets Teddy continue to grow, if he gives her eight, nine more years of marriage. She'd sign up for that.

Eight, nine years, an entire room full of portraits: Teddy holding a red balloon, this unborn child, she and Ethan in their thirties. She'd agree, rip God's pen out of his hand, scribble away right there on the dotted line. Eight, nine years. That's a lot of happiness.

It would be much easier if she knew the precise moment her joy will end. She wouldn't need to worry about Teddy getting hurt, this baby being born without sight, the salesgirl who gave Ethan her card.

You can always spot the girl who wants to fuck your husband. The tall one with the big hello, the one who bothers to remember your name, mentions that they met you at this or that affair. Busy girl, sizing you up, praying her legs are long enough to stretch over you and around your husband's cock.

Sweet girl with the right rings, hip haircut, owner of such a cohesive memory. Sweet girl with that nasty twinkle in your glittering green eyes, kissing my cheek, shaking my hand, saluting me. I'd rather you just fuck me now, in person, here, as you rudely swallow that salty hors d'oeuvre.

Julie is sure that girl is out there somewhere. On the sidelines, one more high-school cheerleader. There she is, skipping over to practice, some dumb jock's varsity jacket. Kick higher, kick higher, baby.

In one week Julie has her big sonogram. From that the doctor will be able to confirm what the baby is. But Julie is already sure that it's a girl. She noticed it the other day. She was walking home, up Columbus with Teddy. *Who is that young lady passing by the window? Yes, you with that absolutely adorable little boy in one hand and that huge chocolate cone in the other.* Julie remembers staring at her reflection in disbelief. Definitely a girl in that belly. How terrifying to be this lucky.

She shuts her eyes and swallows her nausea back down. She will fail a daughter though. Differently than she will fail Teddy, but she will fail her nevertheless.

Of course she will try her best not to. Try to nurture her daughter. Build her into an astronaut, a space shuttle captain. Help rid her of unnecessary guilt. Her daughter should have no inhibition, no sense of what she is or is not allowed. There is almost nothing she won't be allowed. She wants her to fly, live her whole life as if she were able to fly.

Yet in truth these are secondary. Julie circles her stomach with her right hand. What she really wishes for, more than anything other than health, is for her little girl to be pretty. She knows she shouldn't feel this way. But she can't help herself. While pretty may not equal safe, it sure makes it a hell of a lot easier.

So fine, say this baby growing in her belly comes out, say she is the most pink-skinned, rosy-lipped, lovely thing in the world, then what? Will she be able to love her? Is it possible to love the younger, more innocent, more potent version of yourself without envy?

This same rain is tapping against the windowpanes of her new house. The grass is darkening, the air moist. Tap, tap. The entire world is getting ready for spring. Tap, tap tap. Julie checks the clock by the bedside. Her mother must be ready for her date by now. A black stole slung across her shoulders, an alligator bag, two stomach pills, pressed powder and a Tampax. Fifty, this is her fiftieth date with her new face.

"Mama, cowds." Teddy is scampering toward the bed. Julie lifts her body up and switches on the lamp. He is washed and "ready for night-night?"

"No." He is climbing up to show her something he added to their drawing. One foot on the bed frame, he lifts the other leg up and over. He is on the bed, the tips of his feet beneath her sheets. "Pink cowds. Look, Mama, pink cowds."

She is in the present. Her son is snuggled in her arm, reviewing. There are "twees and couds and the sun and fowers an..."

Julie looks at him. His eyes are clear, his skin smooth. His wonderment is absolutely breathtaking. She looks at him talking and pointing. He is a pajama wearer now like his father. And she is the mother.

TWENTY

One by one they are carried out of the apartment. Bits and pieces of her life, of their lives together, are safe, wrapped in bubble, secured with tape. Yesterday's rain has settled into a heavy fog, leaving the day grayer than expected. And wet. Everything about today is wet. Mud is being tracked throughout the apartment by the movers. There are four of them, two to carry out, two to load.

The living room is empty, the kitchen. Teddy sits on the wooden floor next to Georgie. She is reading to him. Ethan is getting the car. Julie is pacing. There is no chair for her to sit on, no pictures to look at, no cigarette to smoke.

"Little guy will need this," the mover says about Teddy's crib as it passes by and leaves their apartment.

"Cib," Teddy calls out, pointing at the mover. The mover is cute, young guy about Julie's age, Jets T-shirt rolled up at the arms, hard chest. Sweating.

The rooms that she and Ethan, that she, Ethan, Teddy, Georgie inhabited only hours ago have been reduced to walls. Thin walls, empty papered space. All the life is gone. It's as if each of her meticulously collected ornaments, now boxed, contain her soul.

The black marker on this box says linens, master bedroom. The next is marked Teddy's toys, little boy's room. Then chintz, china, dining room. One by one the backdrop of her life, the backdrop that she created: pretty wife, young mother, happy pink apartment with an old lunch box collection and teapots and pattern upon pattern of strawberries and yellow-and-green plaid, one by one they are walked out the door.

Julie imagines that this is how it would have been if she died. Ethan's mother and sister packing all but her memory into these same cardboard boxes: Winter coats, front hall closet. Nice girl, just couldn't take it.

The moving truck outside is full and ready to go. All of it, all that Julie had found a commonality with, fabric samples that had turned into couches, antique end tables, twisted brass candlesticks. All of it is loaded and ready to be moved. Julie tips the driver of the truck fifty bucks. They will take a lunch break, meet her at the house in about two hours. Then it will begin again, her life with these things.

Julie has Teddy in her arms. She is helping him wave bye-bye to his bedroom. She wonders what he'll remember of this place. Of the details she had chosen in anticipation of his life.

Now they are in the kitchen. Julie is waving Teddy's arm up and down at the kitchen tile. "Say bye-bye, happy cow."

"Bye-bye."

She'll probably feel bad if Teddy doesn't remember this apartment, but that may actually be better. If he can't remember these kitchen tiles he won't remember the couple of weeks she was gone. Or the past several months she's spent mostly in bed.

She asks Georgie to take Teddy down to the lobby. She will meet them there in a few minutes. She has to double-check before locking the place up, five minutes at the most, tell Ethan not to worry.

Julie looks inside each closet, lifts the lid of the washing machine: empty. Wipes the mud the movers have tracked across the foyer floor. She opens the back door, puts the mop in the waste basket, takes a last look at the stairwell. There is nothing more to do. It is time now to say her own good-bye.

Julie is inside the bathtub, looking up. The shading cast by the temporary pig-tailed lighting makes the paper in the bathroom appear mustard. She touches the faucet with the tip of her sneaker. She looks up again and remembers that she had noticed it then too, the seam in the ceiling paper peeling back.

Dry, there isn't much space. It's funny, she thinks, how shallow this tub actually is. How it couldn't be more than five, five and a half feet long. Two, two and a half feet deep.

This is what Julie knows of the rest of her life. She knows that she picked painted red frames for the picture wall here in this apartment and will have black ash in the new house. She knows that she will sell her formal china and replace them with simple white dishes, slipcover her couch in ivory linen, have the floors stained a dark almost black brown. There won't be a center island in her new kitchen, no reaching over a counter like a short-order cook.

She shuts her eyes. She made two babies in that room out there. Julie turns her hands outward. She slides her palms down the porcelain. There is not much distance. Two or three inches. It is obvious to her now, how small a space this is in which to drown.

She is taking one last look at her view of Central Park. The same view the real-estate broker showed her the first time she and Ethan ever walked into this bedroom. "Stick your head out the window and turn."

Julie's head is out the window. Beneath her she sees the last of her things being loaded onto the truck. She leans out a bit farther and turns her head to the right. Central Park is still there.

Trees, did you notice me?

She is kneeling on the bedroom carpet. The part of the carpet that is shaded where the bed used to be. She is praying. Her hands are clasped in front of her face. She is whimpering before God and the bright pink peonies that surround her. She is thanking them. She is trembling in this final hour.

The Davis family is on the FDR, heading toward the Triborough. The sun is poking itself out from behind the clouds. They will go over the bridge, pay the toll, and head toward the LIE. They will take the LIE to Exit 39. Glen Cove Road north to Northern Boulevard. They will make a left onto 107, then a right. They will follow that road past the country market and the gas station. There they will make a final left, a quick right.

Julie sees a flying truck. You probably haven't seen such a thing as a flying truck. But there it is. A mammoth yellow Home Sweet Home moving truck cascading off the Triborough Bridge. The doors swing open and there is Julie's cute mover in his sweaty Jets T-shirt. He is waving. He is giving her the thumbs-up. He is okay, he is, oh it's a parachute, he is parachuting to safety.

Julie watches as the yellow Home Sweet Home moving truck, her Home Sweet Home moving truck sails through the sky. It begins to descend and although it hits the water hard its splash is less than she expected. All of what she had been up to this very moment has suddenly and painlessly disappeared.

She is delivered.

TWENTY-ONE

Julie pulls up to her neighbor's house, hair combed, black leggings. She's happy to go, how neat, a Tupperware party. Audrey's handwritten invite said: Don't forget to bring Teddy. Fortunate, right? to have a neighbor like this.

And Audrey's home is something else. You can't actually see it from the street but then you drive through these ten-foot-tall gates, lots of swirly ironwork and there it is, a turn-of-this-century French chateau. A massive new construction but gorgeous. All the stonework done by hand. Some old-timers brought over from France. Can you imagine?

This is Julie's third visit and still she can't get over it. So much money. She turns off the engine, helps Teddy and Georgie out of the backseat. They walk toward the house; Teddy holding his mother's hand, Georgie trailing behind them. Julie likes this, the easiness, the fresh air, the manicured front lawn.

Inside is all about Provence, mustard and deep green tones. Heavy clay pottery, walnut, a few hints of maple. Julie drops Teddy and Georgie in the basement playroom. Lots of little kids, lots of nannies, chicken fingers, pizza.

Upstairs in the living room it's an altogether different story. Passed hors d'oeuvres, stuffed mushrooms, baby quiche. Audrey introduces Julie to Melissa, Stacy, Jennifer, Jill, Paige, Anna-Rosa, Laney, Sue. Most are married to brokers, money managers, that sort of thing. It's quite obvious, just the way they say her name even, that Audrey is the queen of the group. Married to a self-made guy with a wildly successful start-up. Lots of clandestine "oohing" over that, envy bordering on awe. Although Anna-Rosa's got herself a doctor. Always nice to have a doctor in the group.

Audrey walks Julie over to some girl sitting by herself on the couch. "This is Amy." Turns out Amy's pregnant with her second, has a little guy in the basement, Sam.

"Jericho Jewish?"

"Yes, Tuesdays and Thursdays."

"Mine too."

How wonderful and so on.

Julie sits down. Amy seems nice enough, pretty casual in jeans and a black T-shirt. Chitter-chat fills the air around them. Did you hear that so-and-so's father just made a fortune? Soda? Not just soda, honey, egg creams. Still a mieskeit though, but better a rich mieskeit than a poor one. Ha, ha, ha.

Amy spreads some cheese onto a cracker and offers it. Julie accepts the gesture, bites down. A miscarriage at thirteen weeks. Really? Yes, blames it on bad help, says if the help cooked, just bothered to give a damn.

Julie can't believe it. She spent her life listening to this kind of gossip. Her mother played bridge, never missed a pattern, never failed her partner. Julie leans in, acts interested. Amy does too, although neither of them add much to the conversation and neither of them, Julie notices, eat the cheese.

She can't be serious, wanting to fuck the Russian pro at the club. She's serious. No. Yes. Does she realize how much she's risking? He's cute but—

"Excuse me, girls." It takes a moment, but everyone stops talking. Audrey's hands are clasped, nice ring, emerald cut. "This is Diana, our very own Tupperware Consultant."

Diana, in her navy blue Ann Taylor suit, turns out to be quite the witty one. "Let me start by telling you girls," no ring but the boundless optimism of a woman needing to sell, "that this is not your mother's Tupperware." Big smile with her delivery. The girls love that: it's not your mother's Tupperware. Clever.

Of course there is an irony to this, to the idea of these women spending the afternoon at a Tupperware party. Most of them must know on some level that it's ridiculous, the whole concept of plastic storage altogether old. Every market has this stuff now, ShopRite, Food Emporium, Kings, aisle four, all the way down on the left, bottom left.

"That's not Tupperware," Diana explains. "You want to be a better mother, you purée your kids' food and store it in Tupperware, not Reynolds, not ClickClack, but the real thing." She stops a second, takes a sip of water. "For those of you fortunate enough to have been raised on Tupperware, it's second nature. For those of you who missed out, here's your chance."

Does anyone else get the joke?

Julie looks around the room, a Prada bag, Gucci loafers, a Rolex watch. No, no one gets the joke. In fact, everyone seems very serious about the whole thing. After all, there is a lot to learn about these various products. Most of the girls cleared their afternoons for this, no rush, already exercised. Their little one is down in the basement, older one won't be home until after three, husband's not back until what, half past eight. Sure, I'll have a wine spritzer.

Julie decides on a two-quart refrigerator pitcher and a pre-packaged assortment of kid things. She fills out a check. Lots of thank-yous fly back and forth between her and Diana. All in all a pleasant enough time, but Julie's tired. She starts with her good-byes: Nice to meet you. Mutual. We should get together. Would love to. Italian? Absolutely, Ethan loves Italian.

Julie's trying her damnedest to fit in. A Prada bag, Gucci loafers, and a Rolex watch. She'll get those things tomorrow. Straightforward, easy to find, one hour at the mall, two at the most. Julie walks over to Audrey, thanks her for the invitation, gives her a hug.

Let's see, what's Audrey wearing? Chaiken and Capone khakis and a white Petit Bateau T-shirt. Kieselstein-Cord belt. Easy. Give Julie a few months to lose the baby weight and after that there will be no stopping her.

She waves to the rest of the group. She can do this. Yes, of course she'll be sure to tell them when the baby comes so they can send her a gift. You don't need to. Yes we do. Okay, okay, thank you.

There is one thing though. That final "Bye bye, honey" laugh that they give. That dumbed-out idiotic, phony fucking laugh is tough. Makes Julie cringe. But if she has to she'll learn to laugh that way too. Really, none of this is out of the ordinary.

Funny, she had sworn she was going to be different than her mother. For instance, she would never wear fur, never live in a big house, never waste away her days lying in bed. Julie was going to do more with her life, help people, volunteer, fundraise.

Sure. Julie laughs. So much for being a do-gooder. Still no fur, but give her time. She turns on the engine and waits for Georgie to buckle Teddy in. "Did he have a good time, Georgie?"

"Yes, ma'am." Georgie smiles, fixes Teddy's jacket. "A great time, ma'am."

Julie pulls past Audrey's Range Rover and a bevy of other luxury cars. She makes a right turn out of her neighbor's driveway and follows it with a sharp right into her own. "Nice house, huh, Georgie?"

"Yes, lucky woman, pretty house."

TWENTY-TWO

Julie sits, hair shorter, darkened nipples slowly filling with a milk she will never use. Her stomach bulges tight around her. Here she sits, head pressed against a pony-skin headboard, waiting. Her child sleeps beside her, old enough to feel her absence if she rises out of this bed they share. Each of his breaths asking her not to leave too soon. Each suggests to her promises she must keep, buried lies, failure. She notices the way his thighs are shaped: wide, strong, sturdy like his father's. There is a slight bruise on one, new, just above the knee. She tries not to wonder.

Teddy's large hands reach out into these early morning shadows and touch her face. His breath close to hers is salty, the pretzels they shared the night before made it pasty, dry. She remembers him as a baby, pure, fresh, almost too clean. Somehow enough time has passed for his breath to mutate into a man's. Still, though, his goodness remains. It's in and around him. Look at him. Lying on his back, his arms spread open in full vulnerability. She stands on the woolen carpet. She hasn't ruined him yet.

Julie sits at her desk filled with a girl. She turns on her happy light. 10,000 LUX of full spectrum light. She reaches for the small jar of sunblock and opens it, applies a dime-size amount to the palm of her hand. She got a bit too red last week but it shouldn't happen again. She begins laughing. This noise of herself, this vacant, taunting, wicked little laugh she hears embarrasses her. Here, in front of this contraption, she wonders what she could possibly want from all this. Here, begging at light, she wonders what it can offer.

This little girl forces her to remember things. The way her father looked at her. His eyes ravaging her with expectation. She's forgiven him, she reminds herself, shutting off the thought. But lately, she wonders, can it be forgiven?

She turns around for a second to check on her sleeping son. It would be so easy to steal from him if she wanted to. An unguarded kiss, a touch not quite right. She could take in small pieces. She could, as her father had, make sure he'd never know what she stole.

What did he steal? In a way nothing. He never made love to her, never touched her in the ways she wanted him to. Didn't she want him to? This is the fuzzy part. How much of whatever happened between them is her fault, her T-shirt too tight, her smile too wide.

There are things she'd like to tell him, angry hateful things. *Ethan's balls are larger than yours, Daddy, really, and he has this great big wand of a cock...*

But it's a sword she spends her life sparring with. Letting him in, spitting him out. A lavish, exhaustive struggle ensues from the depths of her pussy. She keeps Ethan at bay, hovering the perimeter of her soul. *If he can't own me then he can't discard me.*

Julie looks at her belly. Yesterday she bought a pair of earrings at Barneys, twinkly things. She also got her makeup done by some friendly guy behind the Nars counter. He put a shimmer stick above her eyes, defined her cheekbones with bronzer. Teddy sat in his stroller, sucking a lollipop. Such a good boy.

"Look at you." The makeup artist said. "You're gorgeous." When Julie turned and saw herself she looked pretty. She did.

And my baby girl?

Unlike her brother, she will never grow into a man. Never be able to walk away.

"Three more weeks," Ethan says to her over the phone. He calls to check in, to say hello. He understands more now. Every day he states her time as if it were a prison sentence they were both waiting to be released from. "Three more weeks, and you can start taking your medicine again."

But he is out, Julie thinks. In the city. Another guy on his way to work. Dressed in a suit, standing at the corner waiting for the light to change. There he is, lit by an irresistible blue sky. She convinces herself it's easier that he is there. Free from hormones and illusion. She is, she knows, even at twenty-six, a girl still. A girl not quite capable of ever becoming a woman.

What Julie thinks about is this and mostly only about this. She looks up at the light and away again. Foolishly she allowed herself to become barefoot and pregnant. A bad cook in the suburbs of Long Island. Very busy making all sorts of promises over bowls of boxed spaghetti. Forgetting that who she was in that moment of serving was no more than a girl on a respite. Her back a bit straighter. Safely, she learned to cry in the womb of her antidepressant. Mistakenly, from this accomplishment, she thought she had survived.

She turns off her light and returns to their bed. In another fifteen minutes she will wake the little boy for his day. Get him dressed. Fix him breakfast. Drive him to play group. Throughout each of these tasks she smiles, pretending that she's okay. That it's easy for her to beat the eggs, to buckle him into his car seat, to begin.

Julie turns her body into her son's, warming herself against her boy's warmth. She can see out four separate windows from her bed. It's spring. The leaves are blooming and it's time, she thinks, to get over this all.

In truth, she knows what she wants. She wants to become whole and stay whole. She wants to jump up and down and scream, "I'm having my own little girl." Yes, in these early morning shadows there is no misunderstanding her hope. She leans back and feels her daughter, kicking. The mother runs her hand cautiously over her stomach. She shuts her eyes to feel more. How much she wants to want her. How regretful she is that she can't.

TWENTY-THREE

The light is bright against her eyes, and Julie is scared. So scared that it is hard for her to understand what's taking place, although she is totally aware of what's taking place. A hospital attendant with a portable sonogram machine is squeezing warm jelly onto her belly. He circles her stomach with a wand of sorts. The baby's head is down, locked into position.

Another pokes an IV needle into Julie's arm. Drip by drip the Pitocin begins entering her body, causing her to cramp prematurely, causing her to deliver two weeks before she was expected to deliver. It is the middle of July. This baby will be a Cancer.

Dr. Salzman, still in his street clothes, checks her IV. It is seven o'clock in the morning. His appearance is meticulous. He wears a linen sport coat with a cotton oxford, tan shoes that lace up. He's stopping by to review the results of the heart rate monitor. He unrolls the test paper, fine, terrific. Julie notices his wedding band, thin, gold, utterly refined. He has confident hands. Groomed and self-assured. Hands that should be used to catch a baby.

"You remain the perfect candidate for inducement," he says, looking at her with such kindness that she is forced to turn away from him. What does it mean to be a "perfect" candidate for such a thing?

On the floor next to the hospital bed is Julie's overnight bag. In the bag there is a robe, two extra pair of socks, a clean T-shirt, underwear, her hairbrush, and a zippered accessory case. The zippered accessory case holds her toothbrush and toothpaste, a small tube of Vaseline, and a plastic prescription container. Her pills are beneath the container's childproof top, waiting.

Ethan is talking to Dr. Salzman. "So how long do you think it will be?"

"I'd guess three, four hours at the most."

Julie has come with instructions from Dr. Edelman. She is supposed to start the medicine immediately. There will be no breastfeeding this time. She will take the medicine so that she can be ahead of the postpartum depression. This plan has been discussed and re-discussed. She has a disease no different from asthma.

Julie looks out the large window across from her hospital bed. She watches a barge move slowly down the East River toward the Atlantic and can't help but picture her baby floating among the worms and shit inside of her. But Teddy survived living in there and look how beautiful. This baby girl will be released soon. What did Dr. Salzman say? Three, four hours at the most.

It is hot, even though the room has air-conditioning. Julie is starting to feel the contractions. A little cramp and then it's gone. Another little cramp a few minutes later. Three hours doesn't seem long enough to prepare, though. Julie is wearing a cotton hospital gown. She is worried about pain. About the sheer physical pain of it all. She remembers how much the cut hurt with Teddy. His head so large. She touches her breasts. Nothing hurt more than when her milk came in, but this time she's not going to breastfeed. That should make it easier. Two, three weeks and she'll be mostly all dried up.

Dr. Salzman is back in the room, this time in scrubs. He has two C-sections, another vaginal, and then it's Julie's turn. He moves his finger inside of her, asks the nurse for an amnio hook. He sticks what looks like an extra-long crochet needle into her and water comes out. "This should get you going."

Julie's legs are over the side of the bed. "Ow," she says, her stomach cramping. Another doctor, this one named Sandra, is administering her epidural. She is pointing a needle at her back. Ethan is holding Julie's hand. He is asking the anesthesiologist question after question about time, "How long will this take to work?" and pain, "How much will it hurt?" Time and its relation to the distance of her pain.

Julie focuses on the bag next to her bed. It is hard for her to remember herself on the medicine. She likes to think she was prettier, her eyes, the way she smiled.

Ethan sits on the chair next to her and rubs her head. His thumb strokes her forehead and waits and strokes her forehead again. He has been very kind to her throughout this whole pregnancy. He leans over and kisses her. Julie notices the tightness to his smile.

Ethan is still young. And while both of them are young, he's the only one young enough to love. It has been a very long time since Julie was able to love anything, even her son, the way she is being loved by her husband at this moment. "Don't worry," she hears him say as she shuts her eyes.

Her father had visited her the last time she was in a hospital. On his knees, head down, his face pressed into the mattress, he held her newly bandaged arm just above the wrist. She felt his hair brush against her side. She was in intensive care, waiting to be moved to the psych ward. The sedative made it impossible for her to speak. She couldn't offer him anything of herself. So she listened, unsure as to how she should respond, or even if she could respond.

Her father's voice was muffled and broken. He was speaking so softly that she was unsure of what he was saying. But now, after almost a year, she can hear his voice whispering into her ear, "I'm sorry, flower." Again he says this. "I'm sorry, flower." And then again.

Julie remembers wondering how it was possible that she could feel both unbearably sad for him and at the same time feel nothing. She wondered how she had ever loved him. She wondered if after loving him as hard as she did she would ever be able to love anyone else. She wondered how it was that she was still alive.

Ethan pushes her shoulder. "It's time, honey." She opens her eyes and it's time now to "Push," Dr. Salzman instructs. He stands between her legs, wearing a mask. A mirror is extended from the ceiling so Julie can watch the delivery. She is studying the dark, tangled hair around her vagina.

"And, push again."

She is pushing. She is breathing in and pushing as hard as she can.

"Don't be scared to make noise," the doctor says.

But she won't. She will push her little girl into the world silently. Later she will ask for forgiveness, sacrificing any want of her own, any desire for anything other than to continue living. To raise her. To keep her away from uncertain, unscrupulous eyes. She hears her father even now. "I'm sorry, flower."

"I can see her!" Ethan.

"Is that her?" Ethan again.

"It sure is." The doctor.

"Push hard, Julie." The doctor again.

And then there she is.

"She is absolutely perfect, Julie." Dr. Salzman turns the baby toward her mother. The baby girl's head is the size of a small oval coconut.

Ethan watches the nurse carry his daughter to the heater and then turns in the direction of his wife. "She's okay, Julie." He is looking his wife in the eyes. "I saw her whole life as she came through you. I saw her at her prom. She's okay, this little one." He rests his hand on his wife's shoulder. "You don't have to worry, hon."

Julie has tears in her eyes. She wishes her vision could stay this way forever. Refracted by these specific tears so that she could see the world only as it exists in this moment. A world where she is able again to believe in the color pink.

TWENTY-FOUR

They are all gone now, all the visitors, all her family and friends have gone home to sleep. Julie is alone. Alone to care for her daughter in the way God intended. A bottle of unopened formula rests on her bedside table. She is stealing this time, trying to remember all of it, the softness of her baby's rounded cheek as it presses up against her chest. Her pointy nose that of a small bird. Her expansive forehead that of an ancient queen. Her lips a puckered valentine.

Teddy's mouth clamped and pulled. His mouth left her breasts raw and exhausted. This baby latches onto her breast with a steady ease. It's as though she already knows that she has to be gentle with her mother. She is a good little girl.

Julie is filled with an incommunicable regret. She can only do this one time. She watches her daughter's mouth. This baby girl would have been a good breastfeeder.

Julie glances at her overnight bag, still waiting at the right of her bed with her toothbrush and extra socks, with her robe and her pajamas and her zippered accessory case. She forces herself to think back to that day. How easy it is to slip into despair, to feel as if it is all too much. Yes, today is beautiful. As beautiful a day as the day Teddy was born. But she should know by now, she has to know; she does know that what happened last year could happen again.

Dr. Edelman explained that her history makes her even more susceptible to depression. Depression is physiological. It is beyond her control.

Except that it is entirely within her control. The medicine. The medicine that she is supposed to take will provide Julie with a trampoline of sorts. So that when she falls she can only fall so far. On medicine she will be able to determine that the length of most people's arms are, in actuality, too short to harm her.

Her father is kicking her up the stairs. That was how it happened when anger would overcome him. He'd chase her up the stairs and lock her in her room. No, he'd chase her up the stairs, kicking her in the back and then her stomach. She would roll upward. A bounce. A ballet step. Beauty in rage. Rage within beauty.

Julie isn't going to think of this right now. She is tired of her father invading her every moment. After so much time he still meets her this way. In and out of most every thought is his face, the taste of his breath, the sticky sweat that stained the back of the pajamas he wore.

His sleep is heavy, her father's. She can hear him calling out his mother's name. He would call for her, "Mama?" and then there would be snoring, or a chortle and he would roll over and hold her. Julie feels his arms grasping onto her, his penis unknowingly hard against her back. "Mama?" he would ask again.

Julie runs her finger across her baby's eyebrow. She grew up thinking that only the most heartless person could ever leave their child. Yet she tried to leave Teddy. She wonders if abandonment is something in the blood. Another genetic error that will one day be able to be eradicated. The abandonment and adultery gene. The abandonment, adultery, and…

She is lying on her side, looking up at her little girl, swaddled in a plastic bassinet. It is over. This much she knows. Her larger fears have been relieved. The baby is healthy. Ten fingers. Ten toes.

But will the baby feel bonded to her if she doesn't breastfeed? Will she get sick without the immunity of breast milk? Does this make her a bad mother? It's better to breastfeed, every study says so. She looks again at her sleeping baby.

With the help of Dr. Edelman, Julie will learn to navigate herself through this whole not-being-able-to-breastfeed thing. Of course this little girl will feel bonded to her. Who's to say what makes a good mother? Doubt is as debilitating an evil as fear. Julie must force herself to remember this, force herself to have faith.

There is a murmur, an insistent din that echoes throughout the halls of this hospital at night. A nurse calling over the intercom. The trays on the food service cart. A lone television, pattered footsteps, other mothers walking back and forth to the nursery. The smell of whitefish salad seeps into Julie's bedroom. Too many bagel-toting visitors.

A hospital: care being exchanged from stranger to stranger. Julie looks at her daughter one last time before shutting her eyes. She is not going to think of what her life was. She is not going to think of what had been or could have been. She is going to concentrate on what is. Julie rests her hand alongside the bassinet.

This will be her argument: She made it through these nine months and she is okay. So what is an additional six weeks? She will platform. She will throw out statistics. Who's to say that she will even get depressed? The first few weeks, the "baby blues," she can handle. And the heavy depression, if she even gets depressed, doesn't set in until about six weeks. She is practicing the argument. She is asking:

"I'm just asking for six weeks." She pushes away the bagel and coffee Ethan has brought her.

"You can't have them," he says in the most dismissive, matter-of-fact tone.

But you can. You can do whatever you want. I don't tell you how to be her father. Julie is biting her lip. She wants to say these things and then she wants to spit at him.

He stares with disgust at the baby feeding off her breast. He is judging her, his eyes hardened like two still marbles.

"We've discussed this repeatedly. Dr. Edelman and you and me. You can't do it. You have to take the medicine and you can't breastfeed on medicine."

Julie won't look at him. There are moments, and this is one of them, when the difference between a man and a woman is blazingly apparent. He could never understand what it will mean to not provide for her child in this way.

Ethan hasn't had to miss a day of work, a basketball game, nothing. There is no personal sacrifice a man has to make in order to have a baby. And Ethan will continue to live this way. For the rest of their lives he will be able to walk in and out of their front door at his leisure without any penalty. He can stay out all night, call it work, and no one will judge him. There is no stigma attached to a man who doesn't wish to diaper his baby, but a mother who doesn't breastfeed. "I was okay for nine months, Ethan."

He takes her hand and clasps it within his own. "I'm sorry, hon."

They stand in front of the nursery window and watch in utter amazement. Ethan's arm is around Julie. "Look at our little daughter." An RN is giving their baby her first bath, trickling water over her tiny body, her head cupped in the palm of the nurse's hand as if she were a football.

The RN towels their daughter off, combs what amounts to only a few strands of hair, swaddles her in a clean blanket. "All done," she mouths to their daughter, lifting her up for her mother and father to see, waving her tiny fist up and down. Julie can't believe it, this baby, so familiar a stranger.

"Hello, Rachel," she whispers into the glass. "Hello, my brave little girl."

TWENTY-FIVE

Julie is in the backseat of the Explorer, taking Rachel home from the hospital. She is listening to the music on the car stereo and watching Ethan drive. She is chatty, rambling on about who Rachel looks like, about the Batman doll she has for Rachel to give to Teddy, "he'll like that, don't you think?" She is trying to be normal, trying to prove to Ethan that she is together enough to breastfeed.

They're waiting in the den, Teddy, her mother, Georgie, a baby nurse. The baby nurse, Eleanor, will stay for three months. She will tend to all Rachel's needs. She will bathe her, give her the middle-of-the-night feeding. All of this pre-planned, all additional precautions. The aim is for Julie to have a "community of support," as Dr. Edelman called it.

Elenor has already taken Rachel from Julie's arms and carried her off to her room. Teddy is running to his mother. He throws his arms around her neck, thank God, thank God for this boy.

But Julie doesn't want to hold him just yet. The cut between her legs feels raw. She wants to get the smell of the dried blood off her. She unhooks Teddy's arms, kisses his head, and walks up the front stairs to her bathroom.

She sits down slowly on the toilet, hoping that her pee won't burn. She is happy that she chose a white Carrara marble. It's clean in her new house. Clean and white. Her urine stings but only a bit. She squeezes water from a water bottle. Dabs herself with a witch hazel pad.

Julie stands naked before the bathroom mirror. Her breasts swollen, her nipples are large, dark brown, bumpy. She stares at her thighs and wonders how they will ever return to what they were before she gained these forty-two pounds. She is worried that she will not be able to lose this weight without unraveling.

She begins making deals with her reflection. Okay, if taking medicine will really help her keep calm then, fine, she'll take it. She'll take the medicine, allow the nurse to bottle-feed her baby. Everything doesn't, everything shouldn't for that matter, have to be the same for Rachel as it was for Teddy. She will not ask for more than she has already asked for. After all, she is being robbed of very little.

Julie reaches for her medicine, unlocks it, places a pill in her hand. She walks into the shower, lets the hot water scald her back.

Just a month ago she lay on a quilt in her backyard, her boy in the groove of her arm, staring up into the sky. A moon picnic she called it, holding him close to her. She remembers the way the starlight struck Teddy's face, marking his eyes with a translucent all-consuming love. How lucky she felt, that her hormones were keeping her whole, that she hadn't died, that there was this baby in her belly and medicine to take this time, that there was this moon on this night and her little boy.

Julie looks into her hand and sees it, all that moonlight in a little blue pill. *It's oval*, she thinks, *oval, not round*. She glances at her body. It is a discarded vessel, empty, swollen with waste. She already takes up too much space for offering so little.

She tilts her open palm, letting the water carry the pill away. Julie watches it descend, circling at the trap of the drain for a second or two, only to drown.

TWENTY-SIX

Julie is sitting at her vanity. Rachel is lying between her knees. She is watching her mother lift the mascara brush up to her eyelids. The baby girl smiles. There is a dimple on her left cheek beside her mouth. Julie is careful to run the brush evenly through her eyelashes. *She will study me this way her whole life.*

Julie adds a bit more taupe to her eyelids. It seems to her that she is truly all that she ought to be, a young mother dressing for her daughter's baby-naming. She wonders how her little girl will decorate her own eyes. With the stroke of a brush it happens. A bit too much green eye shadow in the crease of your upper eyelid, and you become your mother.

The baby turns inward toward her mother's breast, wanting. Julie looks back at her closed bedroom door. She is safe, she thinks, to do this. She unbuttons her silk blouse, lifts Rachel to her breast. She's been sneaking around this way for nearly two months, misleading Ethan, Dr. Edelman. But at six she'll stop. All the articles seem to agree that if you breastfeed for six months you've given your baby everything he or she needs.

Although if she were smart she'd stop now. Somewhere inside herself she has already acknowledged that she not only should but must stop. She is too edgy with Ethan, with the kids. Like the other night Rachel was crying and it was driving Julie crazy. "Please," she begged, she offered Rachel her breast, bounced her on her shoulder, and still the crying.

At a certain point, maybe three, four minutes into this Julie recognized that she was squeezing Rachel too hard and that this may in fact be the reason for her daughter's incessant crying. Julie's merciless desire to quiet Rachel was rather frightening to her. But she held it together, walked the baby down the hall to the nurse, let her figure it out.

Stopping with the breastfeeding shouldn't be too hard on either of them. It's not like she's giving Rachel every feeding. Mostly the baby is bottle-fed by the nurse. Julie's breast is only one or two times a day. It's impossible to sneak in more with all the people around here watching. *Four more months*, Julie reassures herself as she watches Rachel drink. *Four more months I can do. Four more months is easy.*

Georgie intercoms Julie's bedroom, "The man from the party-rental company is waiting outside; he wants to be paid in cash."

"I'll be right down," Julie answers, shouting in the direction of her phone. She closes her bra. "Sorry for cutting the meal short," she says, kissing Rachel's forehead.

Julie counts out one, two, three hundred for the tent. One, two hundred for the table and chairs. "Thank you," she says, passing the party-rental guy five hundred dollars. She turns and looks out the French doors that lead to the back patio of her house. The tent is situated directly beyond the pool, the bar just through these wooden doors.

Julie walks through the den to the front stairs of her home, her baby girl in her arms, her son gripping her leg. This summer has been good for Teddy. He's taller, his run smoother, he's even able to climb up the ladder on his playground. With a little help, of course. One leg up. A push on his butt, another stair and down the green slide of his jungle gym.

"Stop dragging onto me, hon," Julie says, pulling him off her leg. Her voice comes out sharper than she intended. Teddy's face sinks a little. She's been trying to detach herself from his needs. Wanting to love Rachel as much as she loved him. Wanting to give her daughter every opportunity she gave her brother. But Teddy is clutching the railing, looking toward his mother for direction. His eyes full of need. He is not even two years old. He is also a baby.

She must try to remember him. Make the effort to spend more time with Teddy. To read to him, teach him new words. Julie is simply worn out from worry: who she loves, how she loves, if her love is good enough. Teddy, Ethan, Rachel, Teddy, Ethan, Rachel.

But today is straightforward. Today is about this little baby girl. Feel her trying to lift her head off her mother's shoulders. Teddy will just have to learn that it isn't always about him. In fact, it's a good lesson: how to partake in another's joy. Julie reaches the top of the stairs and turns. "Come, honey," she says to Teddy, reaching out for his hand.

"Georgie, can you come here?" she hollers.

Julie is rushing around Teddy's room. He is squatting on the floor, piling one wooden block on top of the next. Rachel is squirming in her arms. She checks the outfit she laid out on her son's bed earlier in the morning. Teddy's new shoes, brown loafers, are still in their box, rubber soles so he won't trip. Camel pants, clip-on tie.

"That's a great job you're doing," Julie says, holding the tie up to him. Georgie has come from setting his tub. Julie leaves

Georgie to bathe him. She stops at his closet to return the clip-on tie. She looks back; Teddy's arms are around Georgie's neck. She is pulling down his pants. Yes, Julie thinks, turning toward the baby's room. The cotton vest is the right choice for today.

Julie hears the florist's car pull into the driveway. It is nearly fall. A few leaves on the maple just to the left of her front path are already yellowing. She hurries down the hall to Rachel's room. Elenor is watching television. Always the same show. "My religious program" is what she calls it. Twenty-four hours a day of moralizing.

A preacher woman with a light lavender tint to her hair is inviting everyone to pray. Elenor sits straight in her chair, legs crossed, eyeglasses even across her face. "You want me to take her?" Julie places Rachel in her arms. "God have mercy," Elenor says.

Julie stops in the middle of her stairs. She looks up at the light fixture, no dust. She bends her head to the left, and then the right. She takes a breath and looks out the window, past her street and into her neighbor's front lawn. The door of her neighbor's house is open. That's smart, Julie thinks, continuing down the stairs. She turns the knob of her own front door. Opening it. Letting air into her home.

Julie's spent the last few weeks planning for today. She's ordered light pink tablecloths, colorful centerpieces from the finest florist in the area. She's hired a clown to come and twist balloons into little doggies and things like that. There will be a face painter, a cotton candy maker, a moonwalk for the toddlers.

The caterer will serve grilled chicken sandwiches in individual baskets with pink-and-white-checkered tissue. Glass mugs of strawberry soup to start. A thick, moist coconut cake for dessert.

All the Tupperware girls will be here soon with their husbands and their kids. Ethan's family, their kids. David. Her mother is coming with her widower, nice guy, not a bad guy. Her father? Well, forget about her father. Julie takes a second to fuss with her pants. They're pulling slightly at her thighs. She unbuttons the top button. That should do it.

"What smells better than this?" the florist asks, lifting a vase to Julie's nose. "I love a touch of blue sweet peas." Julie waits for the florist to place the arrangements in the center of the table. Then she reaches into the bag she's carrying. It's just a little idea she had, nothing as sophisticated as sweet peas and garden roses. *But how cute are Beanie Babies?*

The first one Julie happens to draw out of her bag is a pink elephant with droopy ears. She smiles. *How cute, so cute. This is terrific, all the kids can take one home.* She puts one on a place setting and waits for the florist's reaction. The professional turns to look. "Adorable," she says.

Julie is happy. This is going to be a nice affair. It's a nice day out, a nice group of people, a nice occasion.

It's always surprising to Julie that people actually come to these things. But here they are, almost everyone she sent an invitation to. The rabbi, the same rabbi who married her and Ethan, who circumcised Teddy, who visited her in the hospital, is holding Rachel up, before God and these seventy-some-odd guests that have filled the backyard of Julie's home.

Julie stands next to her husband. She has lost most of her weight except for the last five pounds, which should drop off as soon as she stops breastfeeding. Ethan is wearing a navy suit. His boy, in his first sport coat, lingers just in front of him. Ethan receives his daughter, swaddled in a lavender blanket, from the rabbi. He holds her comfortably in his arms.

The photographer, same one from their wedding, crouches in front of them. He is pointing his camera, saying, "Say cheese." Julie takes a second to adjust her embroidered shawl in an attempt to conceal her still-fleshy arms, then places her hand on top of Teddy's head and "Smile."

Julie envisions herself turning pages. Her daughter whose baby-naming they are looking at is sitting on her lap, eating a bowl of Breyers vanilla bean ice cream. "Is that you, Mommy?" Julie looks to where her daughter's dainty finger points. She sees herself as she is today: a simple, rather harmless girl smiling within the bound pages of yet another leather photo album.

Julie holds onto Ethan, her arms wrapped loosely around his neck. She moves within his step. She glances over at her brother and winks. Their mother is busy helping Barry with his coffee. You watch, she'll marry him. A wedding at the Pierre, two hundred people, a nine piece band.

Julie can picture her mother carving into a three-tier wedding cake, lifting a full forkful of butter-cream icing to her widower's mouth. In fact, her mother has been quite busy preparing. He should propose no later than a month or two, she'll close the deal fast, a winter wedding with a garden theme: Versailles in spring. She even plans on wearing a wedding gown with a veil. "A peach gown will be nice, don't you think, honey?"

Julie's not quite sure about the peach gown but she is sure that when the time comes her mother will go. She gazes across the dance floor. There is Harriet, busy laughing, obviously quite taken by something Barry just said. There's her mother, anxiously patting some old man's shoulder, flawless manicure, straight across the top, rounded at the sides.

Yeah, Julie thinks as Ethan spins her around, unlike herself her mother will walk freely into a new life: bake Barry her great chocolate cake but a low-cholesterol version, cook him a tender brisket on the holiday. But for the most part that will be all her mother takes from their past. That and whatever residual anger she carries from the divorce, which, granted, may be rather substantial having been betrayed by the man she gave her life to.

But hardly any guilt. Her mother will be able to marry without guilt, which changes the whole proposition. No guilt then very little, if any, shame.

David will walk their mother down this fantasy aisle of freshly planted sod, she'll place one high-heeled foot in front of the other, then again, one high-heeled foot in front of the other. At some point David will be forced to let go, but Harriet will maintain her pace, one high-heeled foot in front of the other, then again. She probably won't turn around to look back at them, not even once, not even a quick wave.

And that will be good, Julie thinks to herself, realizing for what may be the first time that her mother, her seemingly shallow and selfish mother, is above all else a survivor.

TWENTY-SEVEN

The guests are trickling away. Happy women with flower arrangements between their hands. Ethan's favorite Dylan album is playing. Julie looks back at her house, at the newly planted ivy around the fence. The pool they built is so elegant. Grass meeting a simple slate edge.

Julie's arms remain around her husband's shoulders. She is holding on. She is holding on tightly, because by now she is just so tired. Nothing but the smell of mesquite from the grill, nothing but these birds, and these past hours, she will allow nothing other than this moment to fill her head. She is swaying, protected within the cool warmth of this late afternoon air.

Yesterday a woman in the waiting room of Dr. Edelman's office moved away from her when she entered. Julie was wearing a black T-shirt, jeans, new Prada shoes. Nothing at all out of the ordinary. Nothing revealing. Still the lady with the long gray ponytail found it necessary to stand up and move her seat, taking the magazine she was reading and her fruit shake and all her fears of sameness to a chair on the other side of the waiting room.

Julie could sense the woman inspecting her body. First her breasts, then the space between her legs. Julie moved her hand down her cheek, coached herself that the lady's behavior had nothing to do with her, and waited for Dr. Edelman to open her door. Still she can't help but wonder what about her scared this woman. *Did she think I was going to drag her down somehow? Was she scared I was crazy?*

Julie doesn't cry as often as she used to. She doesn't cry like when she first started seeing Dr. Edelman. But she finds herself crying at funny things. Things that you wouldn't think would make her cry, like phone commercials, phone commercials make her cry.

She finds herself apologizing to Dr. Edelman during their sessions. Apologizing for talking about these commercials, Tupperware parties, the wasted time she spends in traffic, commuting back and forth to the city to see her. She worries about the detachment she feels for her son, for her husband, for the baby.

She's scared that Dr. Edelman will ask her to leave her office one day because she is not getting better fast enough. She is scared Dr. Edelman will think she is wallowing. That she is shallow. She is scared that Dr. Edelman will quit on her because she doesn't deserve her patience, does she? After all, Julie hasn't bothered to mention that she's not taking her medicine, that she's breastfeeding, that she's once again a liar.

"I'm sorry if I'm boring you," Julie says. "I know it's ridiculous to cry over pancakes."

It's funny. What she wants hasn't actually changed that much from when she first started seeing Dr. Edelman. Julie wants to go to IHOP. She fantasizes about going there with her father in a white gingham dress, neat bunches in her hair. She wants him to pour IHOP's thick bluebery syrup all over her pancakes and then give her permission to eat them. She wants her eyes back, the eyes she had as a young girl, the eyes she had when she was able to invest faith in a few lousy pancakes.

She knows now that her dad is a runner, and that you can't catch a guy who's running. A guy who gauges his exits on degrees of love. The more you give, the farther he sprints. The more you say *come here*, the quicker he is ready to go.

Julie looks up at the sky above her, pushes her tears back into her eyes. She holds onto Ethan even tighter. He is singing along to a Dylan record.

He is humming into his wife's ear, "I just don't think that I could handle it. Don't fall apart on me tonight..."

Julie looks up at him and waits for his lips to come down and kiss her forehead. Which they do. She looks back to the windows that mark the room of her two napping children. She is part of this somehow. Somehow all of this is hers.

Julie rests her head on Ethan's shoulders and imagines that she is floating. Ethan continues humming the melody, "Yesterday's just a memory. Tomorrow is never what it's supposed to be and I need you, yeah."

He dips Julie back over his arm. She looks up at him and smiles. "I need you," he sings, looking into her eyes.

This could be, she thinks. This must be. This has to be the most glorious moment of her life.

TWENTY-EIGHT

Julie is on the floor of the nursery, cutting. *There is a trick to this. What was it?* Rachel is sleeping just next to her on a quilt. She wears nightgowns. Small cotton dresses with prints. Today she is sleeping in cherries, hot pink cherries with mint green stems. Julie turns the scissors downward. She cuts straight, then edges out and back into a triangle. *Yes, they must touch. That's it.* She remembers her mother telling her, "The hands and feet must touch."

Julie is at the bottom of the paper, rounding the corners. She checks to make sure the heels of the feet are on the folded side of the paper. These will be blondes, blondes in polka-dotted skirts. The next group will be brunettes in Capri pants. Julie is excited. She sees streamers and streamers of little girls hanging from her daughter's ceiling. She can't believe she thought of this. How had she thought of it?

Julie is sitting on the carpet in her daughter's nursery, cutting out paper dolls. She is unfolding them now. She has many groupings. Four, five, six. She has been doing this for an hour. She cuts and colors. She is making progress.

Rachel begins crying. Julie doesn't want to tend to her but there is no one else to do it. She puts down the scissors and lifts her daughter from the ground. Her cry is loud, as it has always been. So quiet is this baby except when she is hungry. Hungry or when her nap is disturbed. Hungry, when her nap is disturbed, or her diaper needs changing. "You must get to know your baby," Elenor said to Julie the day she left for a new case. Three months to the day, a taxicab, her uniform still white.

It doesn't matter, Julie thinks to herself as she carries Rachel over to the changing table. The nurse is gone now. Gone. Good. And it really doesn't matter now, does it, what the lady thought of her? *As if I didn't know my baby.* Julie lifts the baby's nightgown up over her legs and opens the diaper.

"There's nothing in here, sweetie." Julie's voice is deliberately slow and cheery. She is trying to calm her daughter down. But Rachel's cry is insistent, and it scares her. Julie looks toward the phone. Should she call the pediatrician? Ethan's cell? No. Ethan and Teddy will be home soon. She can handle this. It's hunger.

Julie checks her watch. It has only been two hours since the baby's last feeding. But she is sure of this; she is certain that the baby is crying out of hunger. She sits on the rocker, lifts her shirt and places Rachel against her breast. But Rachel won't latch on. She grows hysterical, thrashing her head from side to side. "Never mind," Julie says and stands.

Julie makes her way down the stairs. They are carpeted in a nice wool sisal. The baby in her arms is long and narrow. Julie presses Rachel's head against her shoulder. She passes the wooden console at the foot of the steps. There are pictures of all of them there, the family that inhabits this house. She focuses on a recent one of her boy. He is Superman, Superman on a swing-set. Julie glances at this picture of this baby's brother and continues toward the kitchen, tapping her daughter on the back.

Julie will give her a bottle. Elenor gave Rachel a bottle. A bottle, a nipple, a bottle top. Julie pours the water, one, two, three, four ounces. She takes the powder, one scoop, two. She is shaking the formula. Rachel is loud, really loud. "It's coming," Julie says.

But the baby won't take it. Why won't she take it? The baby is squirming as if she instinctively knows to pull away from her mother. "Come on."

Julie sits in a kitchen chair. She holds Rachel on her lap, a diaper cloth over her chest. She is doing everything she is supposed to be doing. But Rachel is still crying. She is squirming and crying and her cry is growing louder. It is too loud, too incessant, too demanding. The noise is hurting Julie's head and "I can't take this," she hears herself say. "I can't."

Julie pushes the bottle in. She is pushing it in. Rachel is turning and twisting. She is making it impossible for her mother. "Dammit."

Julie is thinking of the paper dolls. She is looking at her daughter and thinking, *I don't want to be doing this.* She is thinking, *I want to be hanging those dolls from your ceiling.*

She is saying, "Please stop crying. Please stop crying." She is trying to quiet her daughter, bouncing Rachel on her knee. She looks at the clock on the kitchen wall. Why are Ethan and Teddy staying out so long?

Julie is pacing around the kitchen. She is bouncing the baby and still there is crying. She will force Rachel to drink. She knows this will make her feel better. Rachel needs food. She is the mother and she knows what her baby needs. Again, Julie sits, aims the bottle at her tiny lips. She is pushing it in. Rachel is struggling with her mother but the bottle is in, the crying has stopped. Julie shuts her eyes as her daughter drinks and begins planning.

She will burp Rachel and then change her. They will both be ready when the boys come home. Julie is trying to laugh at herself. *How silly. What was the panic?* "What was that panic, baby?" Julie waits for a response. But the baby is swallowing. *They don't even know,* she thinks to herself.

Julie is looking at Rachel's hair. She can't get over it, that this baby has such light hair. Of all things. And her eyelashes are growing. They are long, even. Her nose is more rounded now than pointed. Rachel spits out the bottle. Julie looks at her mouth and *what is that?* Julie puts the bottle on the kitchen table. She pulls back the baby's lower lip. There is a tiny horizontal opening there. The red is blood.

Rachel is crying again. Something is wrong again. Rachel won't stop crying and her lip is bleeding and "I'm sorry." Julie is begging her to stop. She is running water from the tap. She's begging with words like "shush" and "please."

But the water is too cold and Rachel calls out. Julie turns on the hot faucet. She is bouncing her daughter. She is waiting for the water to warm to the right temperature. Warm water and yes, the blood will wash away. It was an honest mistake. What happened was she pressed the nipple too hard against Rachael's lips. Ethan and Teddy will be home soon and she'll explain everything that happened, how she was cutting out paper dolls and Rachel woke and she wouldn't stop crying and…

Julie is holding her daughter's head under the faucet. A few more minutes and the blood will stop. A few days and the cut will disappear. But this is it. She will tell Ethan the truth. Sundays are too long for her. She needs a Sunday girl. She won't feel embarrassed to tell him that she needs a Sunday girl or that he needs to stay and help her with the baby on Sundays. She has to count on him. But he'll say, "What have I been doing?" He'll say, "Look, I wasn't out playing basketball. I was taking Teddy to get a haircut."

It doesn't matter. Julie needs to know that he won't leave her like this again. She needs to admit that she can't handle this. She can't handle the crying. Rachel's crying makes her too nervous. This makes her a bad mother, doesn't it? No. No, she tells herself as she checks the temperature of the water. It makes her a good mother. She is a better mother for acknowledging her needs. She doesn't need to be alone with Rachel to know her, doesn't need to breastfeed her daughter, doesn't need to earn her love. She just needs to not be scared. If Julie has learned anything she has learned that she has to not be scared. Not be scared to love. Not be scared to be cared for. Not be scared to ask for help.

Julie is holding Rachel's head under the running water. A few more minutes and the blood will be washed away. A few more minutes and there is nothing, no noise, nothing.

The baby was a small baby. Maybe three, four months old. And the baby was a girl. You can tell she was a girl because she is wearing a tiny little nightgown with hot-pink cherries and mint green stems. The mother is holding her, not understanding. She begins shaking her. She is standing over her kitchen sink. The backsplash, a reissue of an old Malibu tile, olive green with a black design.

Some door inside the mother swings open. Seized and unhinged. She is making a noise now. It is an awful noise.

TWENTY-NINE

She is now to any casual observer simply another young, tall-ishly attractive girl in a pair of jeans and a black T-shirt, walking across her backyard. A small baby rests between her arms. The mother's long hair, which is usually pulled back into a neat pony-tail, is loose. She is walking on grass dampened by sprinklers, wearing only socks.

Her eyes are blue. Much more blue than the average person and if you were to see her, walking toward her pool, late in this early fall afternoon, you might stop. Because there is something so reaffirming about this sight. A young mother, her long hair out, down past her shoulders, and she's walking, walking with her little baby, and the neighbor's gardener is blowing the few leaves that have fallen into a pile. It is almost the girl's favorite time of year. The time when the world becomes orange.

A few children from the neighborhood are outside. Through the din of the gardener's blower she can hear them calling each other. A boy is riding his bike; his sister is walking beside him. They stop at the edge of their driveway so she can fix him.

They will travel to the end of the street. A girl with her younger brother. She will hold the bucket as they pick them up off the ground. One, then the next. They have a plan. They are going to sell acorns.

They are laughing because he still has trouble with the pedals. Even though she has papered them for him, his feet sometimes slip off the bottom pedal before it turns back up. She is walking behind, pushing her brother along.

The young mother is aware, even all these years before now, that this moment, this happiness, is something borrowed. Acorns for sale—one cent. It's better than lemonade.

Our girl keeps walking. She is taking off her socks with her feet. She is unbuttoning her pants. She is holding her small limp baby tight against her chest. She is walking one foot in front of the other. She is not thinking any thought now. She is simply moving forward.

The bottom of the pool is rough and scratches her feet. She turns one last time to look at her pretty little house. The shutters, now a periwinkle blue, are the same color as the sky. She looks up. A plane is flying overhead. It is low and loud. It will be landing in LaGuardia in less than fifteen, no, it will be landing at LaGuardia in less than ten minutes.

She thinks of the families coming off that plane. All different kinds of families. In there somewhere is a mother smiling and zipping her child's sweatshirt. She pictures her son, takes one last breath and then submerges herself and her little girl into the cold.

THIRTY

The boy, from the picture on the console. The boy Superman is walking next to a man. The boy is wearing a yellow polo shirt and shorts. They are laughing because they each have an ice cream and because they often laugh like this. For no other reason than the boy is learning how to say things. Which makes the man laugh. And when the man laughs, the boy laughs. Today the boy is repeating the names of the Knicks' starting lineup. He is saying Patrick Ewing. "Patwik Ewing." This is how it happens for these two. This kind of laughter.

He is a man with his son. He is walking around the side of the house to the pool because he promised to take his son swimming. The boy and father were getting their hair cut at the barbershop in town and the boy was so good, all tall in his booster seat, that the man agreed to take his son for a swim. And even though it is a little cool and the boy's mother will be in a panic, he is going to keep his word. The pool will be closing within a day or two, so why not? The man will keep a towel ready at the edge of the steps and bundle the boy up, so he doesn't catch a chill.

They continue. Their haircuts are almost as identical as their walks. But the boy has his mother's eyes. It's uncanny. The same shade of blue. The same pinching at the edges. The same long black lashes.

The man also has a daughter. A three-month-old baby he is just getting to know. A little redhead. His wife is always telling him how much the baby looks like him. But she doesn't. Maybe a little, but mostly she looks like her mother. He pictures his wife and his daughter and smiles.

He is walking, his arm linked within his son's. He is a young man, thirty, thirty-two. It's hard to tell with his new haircut so boyish. He is dressed in jeans and a Nike T-shirt. He is a man like any other man. A man who loves his family although at times he can't quite figure out how all this happened. How he became a man with a wife, a son, a house, a daughter, a pool. But it's okay. The pressure of it all is worth it. He looks up at the sky, gets his son's attention, and points his finger at the plane flying overhead. His father had done these things. Had pointed his finger toward the sky, had taught him how to swim.

The man opens the gate to his backyard and says, "I'll race you to your floaties, son." And they run.

AFTERWORD

by Adrienne Miller

When *A Mouthful of Air* first appeared twenty years ago, our culture wasn't as open about discussing mental health issues as we are today. In the nineties, postpartum depression was generally considered too dark, too frightening a topic to approach in literature, and Amy Koppelman fought for three years to get her powerful and deeply personal first novel published. She hoped Julie's tragic story would serve as a cautionary tale, a warning, and a call to action. Society is still poorly equipped to deal with women's mental health. But it is also true that there has been a reduction of stigma regarding depression, particularly postpartum mood disorders, which affect one in five women. There is substantially more support available now to women who suffer from PPD, and in 2010, the MOTHERS Act, the first piece of federal legislation designed to study and treat postpartum depression, became law.

Still, the idea of being a perfect mother persists. As the mother of a young child, I know all too well the tendency to torture ourselves with exactly this worry. But what is routine, run-of-the-mill anxiety to a psychologically healthy person, becomes, for a clinically depressed person, a thought prison. Julie, the protagonist in *A Mouthful of Air,* ruminates endlessly, repeating the "good mother" line to herself so frequently that it nearly becomes an incantation. *I am a good mother. I am a good mother.* But what *is* a good mother? She purees her baby's food. She cuts out elaborate paper dolls to string up around her baby's nursery. She must breastfeed for at least six months, even when doing so means quitting her antidepressants, a catastrophe that results in the book's final tragedy.

Julie is a wealthy white woman, and her depression can't be connected to overwork, financial challenge, or social injustice. Koppelman's intention here is clear: she is presenting depression as an illness, unrelated to circumstance. Julie recognizes her extreme privilege, an understanding that only reinforces her self-loathing. Does she even have any right to be unhappy? She's lucky, so how can she possibly suffer? Scant mention is made of Julie's life before marriage and motherhood, since her past existence is, evidently, of no consequence. She's now a stay-at-home mother—but with a nanny. (In one of the bleaker observations in the book, Julie considers how pleased she is to be a housewife.) She is spoiled, and ungrateful, and she knows it. And this belief only reinforces what she already knows: the world is better off without her in it.

In addition to the luxury of employing a nanny, Julie also has a well-meaning—though remarkably ineffectual—support group, and it's striking to note how utterly incapable of dealing with her depression the people closest to her are. They're unwilling—unable—to talk about her suicide attempt, and her husband, Ethan, minimizes the act by calling it an "accident." Ethan is loving, he's tender, but he, like most others in the book, treats Julie like a child. He infantilizes her by calling her "Tiny" and "Baby," underscoring her dependence and powerlessness.

Indeed, Julie is one of the most passive characters I've ever encountered in a novel. "Let him determine whether or not she is a fit enough specimen for the task at hand," she thinks of Ethan when contemplating her second pregnancy. She has no power, no voice, no agency, and, crucially, no job. She is creatively and intellectually severed. Her life borders on imprisonment. She sees herself enacting a series of roles: mother, wife, daughter, sister... but who is *she*? Does she even have a "self" at all? Koppelman, with great skill and insight, conveys the grim stasis of a mind on the brink, a psyche caught in gothic cul-de-sacs of thought.

In fact, the work this most closely resembles is "The Yellow Wallpaper" by Charlotte Perkins Gilman. Like that classic feminist horror story, *A Mouthful of Air* also deals with the consequences of living a life of total confinement. In both works, women are trapped: by severe depression, by marriage, by motherhood. The wallpaper of the Gilman classic may be hideously bloated with yellow curves and flourishes, and Koppelman gives us wallpaper printed with bright red strawberries, but her novel is an equally effective horror tale.

In addition to asking what it means to be a good mother, Koppelman's novel poses the fundamental questions, "What is the role of women in society? And how do women find their way?" As with "The Yellow Wallpaper," the implication in *A Mouthful of Air* is that Julie has been driven to all this. So much in society is organized around the perfection of the mother-child bond, yet many of the messages about the mythology of childbearing and child-rearing are simply untrue for a great many women. Surely Julie's depression must be, in part, a symptom of the persuasiveness and oppressiveness of such sexist thinking (*that* is what's behind the wallpaper), but because Julie is so sick, so entombed in spirals of negative thought, the sickness and the sexism become inseparable.

No wonder it was difficult for *A Mouthful of Air* to find a publisher. At the beginning of the novel, we meet a young woman after a failed suicide attempt, though her illness has (temporarily) stabilized. But by the end of the book, the illness has defeated her. It's a difficult book. Fortunately, some wonderful independent presses are willing to take a chance on risky literature that speaks to so many. Suicide rates, regretfully, have risen terribly in the past two decades, and depression is now the leading cause of disability worldwide. We still have a long way to go.

There's nothing easy about being a mother, and there's nothing easy about knowing that the world will, eventually, hurt your child in ways both subtle and profound. Yet, to raise a child, to educate him and be his first teacher—it's an almost unbearable thrill. Nothing in life can prepare you for how terrifying and delightful having a child is. And nothing can prepare you for the knowledge that, in parenting, terror and delight turn out to be the same thing.

ADRIENNE MILLER is the author of the novel *The Coast of Akron* and the memoir *In the Land of Men*. She was the literary editor of *Esquire*.

Two Dollar Radio
Books too loud to Ignore

ALSO AVAILABLE Here are some other titles you might want to dig into.

I SMILE BACK
A NOVEL BY AMY KOPPELMAN

Now a major motion picture starring
Sarah Silverman and Josh Charles!

I Smile Back tells the story of a woman pushing herself to the brink. Married with kids, Laney Brooks takes the drugs she wants, sleeps with the men she wants, disappears when she wants. Now, with the destruction of her family looming and temptation everywhere, Laney makes one last desperate attempt at redemption. Told with haunting, prismatic prose, *I Smile Back* is a raw portrait of a troubled woman struggling desperately to hold on to those she loves the most.

"This crushing novel by the author of *A Mouthful of Air* is a shocking portrait of suburban ennui gone horribly awry. Koppelman's prose style is understated and crackling; each sentence is laden with a foreboding sense of menace. Like a crime scene or a flaming car wreck, it becomes impossible not to stare."
—PUBLISHERS WEEKLY

"Powerful. Koppelman's instincts help her navigate these choppy waters with inventiveness and integrity."
—PAUL KOLSBY, *LOS ANGELES TIMES*

"Laney Brooks is a woman in agony, suffering from an undefined malady that makes standard housewife ennui—boredom from carpooling or picking up dry cleaning—look like a picnic. Laney's despair, [is] ably depicted by Amy Koppelman in her affecting second novel."
—SARA IVRY, *BOOKFORUM*

Books to read!

BORN INTO THIS STORIES ADAM THOMPSON

→ "With its wit, intelligence and restless exploration of the parameters of race and place, Thompson's debut collection is a welcome addition to the canon of Indigenous Australian writers."—Thuy On, *The Guardian*

→ "A compelling new voice, tough yet tender, from the heart of Aboriginal Tasmania." —Melissa Lucashenko, author of *Too Much Lip*

THE REMARKABLE STORIES IN *Born into This* are eye-opening, razor-sharp, and entertaining, often all at once.

A DOOR BEHIND A DOOR NOVEL YELENA MOSKOVICH

→ "It's like a hornier, more visceral *The Crying of Lot 49*." —Kate Zambreno, author of *Screen Tests, Heroines,* and *Green Girl*

→ "The dynamic style and psychological depth make this an engaging mind bender." —*Publishers Weekly*

FROM THE AUTHOR OF THE NATASHAS AND VIRTUOSO comes a "phantasmagoria about immigration, death, and queer desire." (Kat Solomon, *Chicago Review of Books*)

NIGHT ROOMS ESSAYS GINA NUTT

→ "Together, these pieces form an experience that is sensory, intellectual and emotional, illuminating difficult and even uncomfortable truths." —Julia Kastner, *Shelf Awareness*

NIGHT ROOMS IS A POETIC, INTIMATE collection of personal essays that weaves together fragmented images from horror films and cultural tropes to meditate on anxiety and depression, suicide, body image, identity, grief, and survival.

THE HARE NOVEL MELANIE FINN

← "[A] brooding feminist thriller." —*New York Times*

← "Finn has a gift for weaving existential and political concerns through tautly paced prose." —Molly Young, *Vulture*

AN ASTOUNDING NEW LITERARY THRILLER from a celebrated author at the height of her storytelling prowess, *The Hare* bravely considers a woman's inherent sense of obligation—sexual and emotional—to the male hierarchy.

A HISTORY OF MY BRIEF BODY
ESSAYS BILLY-RAY BELCOURT

→ **Lambda Literary Award, Finalist.**

← "Stunning... Happiness, this beautiful book says, is the ultimate act of resistance." —Michelle Hart, *O, The Oprah Magazine*

A BRAVE, RAW, AND fiercely intelligent collection of essays and vignettes on grief, colonial violence, joy, love, and queerness.

Books to read!

ALLIGATOR & OTHER STORIES STORIES DIMA ALZAYAT

→ PEN/Robert W. Bingham Award for Debut Short Story Collection, longlist.
→ Swansea University Dylan Thomas Prize 2021, shortlist.
← "A stellar debut... Alzayat manages to execute a short but thoughtful meditation on the spectrum of race in America from Jackson's presidency to present." —Colin Groundwater, *GQ*

THE AWARD-WINNING STORIES in Dima Alzayat's collection are luminous and tender, rich and relatable, chronicling a sense of displacement through everyday scenarios.

WHITEOUT CONDITIONS NOVEL TARIQ SHAH

← "*Whiteout Conditions* is both disorienting and visceral, hilarious and heartbreaking." —Michael Welch, *Chicago Review of Books*

IN THE DEPTHS OF A BRUTAL Midwest winter, Ant rides with Vince through the falling snow to Ray's funeral, an event that has been accruing a sense of consequence. With a poet's sensibility, Shah navigates the murky responsibilities of adulthood, grief, toxic masculinity, and the tragedy of revenge in this haunting Midwestern noir.

VIRTUOSO NOVEL YELENA MOSKOVICH

→ Longlisted for the Swansea University Dylan Thomas Prize
← "A bold feminist novel." —Katharine Coldiron, *Times Literary Supplement*
← "*Virtuoso* is powerfully mysterious and deeply insightful."
—Nadia Beard, *Los Angeles Review of Books*

WITH A DISTINCTIVE PROSE FLAIR and spellbinding vision, a story of love, loss, and self-discovery that heralds Yelena Moskovich as a brilliant and one-of-a-kind visionary.

SOME OF US ARE VERY HUNGRY NOW
ESSAYS ANDRE PERRY

→ Best Books 2019: *Pop Matters*
← "A complete, deep, satisfying read." —Gabino Iglesias, NPR

ANDRE PERRY'S DEBUT COLLECTION of personal essays travels from Washington DC to Iowa City to Hong Kong in search of both individual and national identity while displaying tenderness and a disarming honesty.

SAVAGE GODS MEMOIR PAUL KINGSNORTH

→ A Best Book of 2019 —*The Guardian*
← "[*Savage Gods* is] a wail sent up from the heart of one of the intractable problems of the human condition: real change comes only from crisis, and crisis always involves loss."
—Ellie Robins, *Los Angeles Review of Books*

SAVAGE GODS ASKS, can words ever paint the truth of the world—or are they part of the great lie which is killing it?

Books to read!

Now available at **TWODOLLARRADIO.com** or your favorite bookseller.

THE BOOK OF X NOVEL SARAH ROSE ETTER

→ **Winner of the 2019 Shirley Jackson Awards for Novel**
→ **A Best Book of 2019** —*Vulture, Entropy, Buzzfeed, Thrillist*
← "Etter brilliantly, viciously lays bare what it means to be a woman in the world." —Roxane Gay

A SURREAL EXPLORATION OF ONE WOMAN'S LIFE and death against a landscape of meat, office desks, and bad men.

TRIANGULUM NOVEL MASANDE NTSHANGA

→ **2020 Nomo Awards Shortlist**
→ **A Best Book of 2019** —*LitReactor, Entropy*
← "Magnificently disorienting and meticulously constructed."
—Tobias Carroll, Tor.com

AN AMBITIOUS, OFTEN PHILOSOPHICAL AND GENRE-BENDING NOVEL that covers a period of over 40 years in South Africa's recent past and near future.

THE WORD FOR WOMAN IS WILDERNESS
NOVEL ABI ANDREWS

← "Unlike any published work I have read, in ways that are beguiling, audacious…" —Sarah Moss, *The Guardian*

THIS IS A NEW KIND OF NATURE WRITING — one that crosses fiction with science writing and puts gender politics at the center of the landscape.

AWAY! AWAY! NOVEL JANA BEŇOVÁ
TRANSLATED BY JANET LIVINGSTONE

→ **Winner of the European Union Prize for Literature**
← "Beňová's short, fast novels are a revolution against normality. "
—Austrian Broadcasting Corporation, ORF

WITH MAGNETIC, SPARKLING PROSE, Beňová delivers a lively mosaic that ruminates on human relationships, our greatest fears and desires.

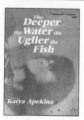

THE DEEPER THE WATER THE UGLIER
THE FISH NOVEL KATYA APEKINA

→ **2018 *Los Angeles Times* Book Prize Finalist**
→ **A Best Book of 2018** —*Kirkus, BuzzFeed, Entropy, LitReactor, LitHub*
← "Nothing short of gorgeous." —Michael Schaub, NPR

POWERFULLY CAPTURES THE QUIET TORMENT of two sisters craving the attention of a parent they can't, and shouldn't, have to themselves.